FISHER CROWN OF ACORNS

**Hodder
Children's
Books**

A division of Hachette Children's Books

In memoriam
John Wood.

The Design

I began to turn my thoughts towards the Improvement of the City by Building.

Bladud

Stop now. To go further is dangerous.
The circle is the oldest magic.
If you enter it it will enfold you.

My name was forbidden. No one spoke its syllables to me
any more. No one touched me, or held me close. Can you
imagine that, you who live far away round the ring of years?
If a man is ill, that's bad enough. But if a king falls sick, his
kingdom is blighted, and he is responsible.
At first I felt itchy and fevered. I was given every care. But as
the moon waned the marks of the disease became clear,
erupting in boils and pustules on my skin.
Sacrifices were made, omens consulted. The stones told me
what had to be done.
I chose a moonless night, and when it was darkest I rose from
my bed and walked away from my kingdom.
My people came out to watch me go.
They made two lines across the downs; they muffled their

3

faces against fear. My wife, my children avoided me with horror.

I was an outcast.

A ghost under the moon.

Far from the peoples of the circles I crept, not coming close enough for them to see the ruin of my face.

How many months I lay in the dead leaves I don't know. Without the circles, there is no time and no way of measuring.

My clothes withered to rags.

My skin was torn with scratches, seeping with pus. I was a contagion, a leprosy in my own land. I was a king and a druid and a man about to die.

I needed a miracle.

And I found one.

Sulis

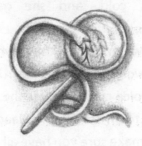

The pale purple bag Alison had bought her in Sheffield was on her lap and she looked out at the perfect city where she would be healed.

The train window was grimy, but through it she could see how the buildings climbed the hill, how all their spires and curved terraces and wide streets were cut from the same buttery, honey-gold stone. Precise. Beautiful.

Opposite, Alison watched. 'Is it like you thought?'

'Better. Much better.'

'There are Roman remains under parts of it, aren't there?'

She nodded, her eyes on her reflection in the glass. 'Springs of hot water. The temple of a goddess.' She'd spent an afternoon in the library in Sheffield, finding out.

Alison laughed. 'You've done your homework then.'

She frowned. Alison often pretended to be ignorant, just a dull social worker who knew nothing. It was always annoying.

'The Romans called the city Aquae Sulis. The waters of Sulis. That was the name of the goddess.' Her voice was cold, and she gave Alison her expressionless look.

Alison's eyes widened. 'So that's where you got the name from. No wonder I'd never heard of it.'

The guard's voice crackled over the tannoy. 'Change here for stations to Bristol Temple Meads and stations to Taunton. Please make sure you have all your belongings, and mind the gap as you leave the train.'

She stood, feeling tension in her stomach as she swung the bag over her shoulder. Alison squeezed past a man reading *The Times* and hauled the two suitcases down from the rack with strong hands, carrying them awkwardly sideways in the narrow aisle.

The train slowed along a long platform. She saw that even the station was golden, behind its advertisements for films and books, its coffee bar. Her mouth was dry. Her hands itched.

Alison's perfume was sweet and cloying, and the whole line of standing people lurched in unison as the train stopped. The doors unlocked with a crack that made her jump and stare at the glass, thinking a stone had been flung.

But the window was whole, and smooth.

And then they were stepping down on to the platform, into a crowd of impatient people who pushed past her and took no notice of her, and there were new noises and a breeze and she breathed it all in deep, the smoky railway smell, the wafts of coffee. Girls ran and hugged. A man said 'the utmost harmony and balance' into a mobile phone as he walked by.

Alison turned. 'All right?'

'Fine.' She pulled the rucksack over her shoulder. She'd keep the joy and the fear secret, hidden deep inside.

They went down some steps and into the booking hall. It was nowhere near as busy as Sheffield. A few people stood in queues for tickets, but when the crowd from the train had streamed out into the street it was almost quiet.

'No sign of them.' Alison frowned; the little lines on her forehead were deep. She dumped the suitcases by the wall. 'They said they'd be here to meet us. I'll check if they're outside.'

When Alison was gone she felt awkward, just standing there. Her eyes were alert, trying to take in everything, but you couldn't, could you, there was too much, and before she realized the old anxiety had come back, and she was watching people to see if they were looking at her face, if they recognized her. Stupid! She turned away, took a deep breath, closed her eyes.

They don't know you. No one is looking at you. You're safe. This is a new life. You're a new person. Dr Malory's voice was calm in her head. She opened her eyes and read the posters on the wall. One of them was a tourist ad for Stonehenge. SEE THE GREATEST STONE CIRCLE IN

BRITAIN! It showed the famous megaliths under a wide blue sky. She read it three times. Then she pulled out her sunglasses and put them on.

'I knew they'd be late! I distinctly said four thirty!' Alison was back, with a faint sweat on her dark skin, hauling up the cases. 'Come on. We'll wait outside.'

Taxies were lined up in the small forecourt. She could have jumped in one. She could have gone anywhere. The drivers looked at her, but it was all right. They were only looking for a fare. They saw a black woman in a suit and a grungy student. They didn't see *her*. She was invisible.

Alison had the mobile out but it was obvious by her face that there was no answer. 'This is a real pain. I have to get the train back in twenty minutes . . .'

'Then go. I'll be fine.'

Alison glared. 'You know I can't do that. I have to be here with you till they come.'

'Hand me over personally.'

'Listen, M—'

'Deliver me, like a parcel.'

She liked to tease Alison. Torment her. Alison knew, because she said, 'You just have to have a go, don't you?' Then her eyes widened and she snapped the phone shut and smiled in relief. 'Here they are.'

They came almost at a run, through the cars, and they were exactly as she remembered from the interview, and the visit to the zoo.

8

Hannah's blonde hair was tied up in a blue and orange wisp of scarf. She wore a print tea dress and a pale green cardigan. 'Oh God,' she said, 'we're so sorry! The traffic.'

Simon wore a hooded jacket and jeans with deliberate holes in them. He was older, his hair threaded with grey. Forty, even. Trying to look young. 'Hi,' he said.

She smiled. 'Hi.'

Alison shook their hands. Suddenly it all seemed a bit formal, and they stood looking at each other among the taxis. Then Simon came forward and kissed her on both cheeks, and she smelt his woody aftershave, and it felt strange. Hannah did it too. Her lips were cool. 'Have you decided on a name?'

She stepped back. 'Yes.'

Alison scowled. 'She could have had any name in the world and she's picked one that will make her stand out a mile! The whole idea of being here is to be inconspicuous. To be safe.'

'I'm having it and you can't stop me.' She turned to her new foster-parents. 'From now on,' she said, 'you must call me Sulis.'

They took it fairly well. Hannah laughed, a nervous, surprised laugh, and Simon put his head on one side and considered. 'Why not? Maybe it's the sort of name we'd have chosen for our kids. Don't you think so? A bit out of the ordinary. A bit hippy.'

Sulis thought so. She had known as soon as she'd first

9

seen them that the new name couldn't be boring, invisible. 'The best way to hide,' she said, 'is not to hide at all. Don't you think?'

'Are you sure?'

'I like it. And you can always shorten it to Su.'

Simon nodded, as if the decision had been his. He said, 'Right. Sulis it is. You'll come back for some tea, Mrs West?'

'I can't, I'm afraid.' Alison put on her regretful look. 'I have to get back on the next train.' She glanced round uneasily. 'Can we go somewhere a bit more out of sight?'

'Car's round the corner,' Simon said quickly. He picked up the suitcases and walked off, not looking back. They trailed after him. To Sulis's surprise Hannah slid a furtive arm around her shoulders and squeezed. 'We're so pleased to have you with us,' she whispered. 'We're all going to get along fine, I can tell.'

Sulis smiled. She'd heard that often enough.

Squashed into the back of the car, Alison delved into her briefcase. She pulled out a large envelope. 'It's all in here. Passport and birth certificate in the new name. National Insurance. Health records. Everything you need.'

Simon said, 'Photographs?'

'Of her from a baby, with both of you. The technicians did them, mixed you in digitally or something. School reports . . . well, you'll see. There's also a contact number with our department, but that's to be used in emergencies only. The local social services and police have liaison officers – their numbers are in there too. They'll be in touch.'

Sulis scowled. 'New life, you said. I thought that meant no more social workers.'

'Yes, but you have to understand . . .'

'Oh, I *understand*.' She turned and stared out of the car window. On the opposite pavement a man sat in the window of a cafe, drinking from a white cup. He stared at her, and she put the sunglasses on again, hastily. 'You've gone through it often enough.'

Alison swapped a pained look with Simon. 'When you're eighteen, M— Sulis, you can do what you like and you know that. Three months, that's all. Until then, you're still our responsibility.'

'Fine.' She wondered if there would be some sort of surveillance on her. How would she know? Maybe the man in the cafe was one of them. But he was already gone, paying for his meal at the till.

Alison slid to the end of the warm seat. 'Goodbye then, love, and good luck. Have a great life. Don't let the past spoil it for you.'

They hugged. Sulis felt the woman's soft body squash against her, smelt the Chanel she always wore. She was surprised at the sudden pang of remorse that came over her. She'd never been that fond of Alison. Of all the social workers she'd known – and there had been dozens

11

– none of them had ever been a real friend. But as the woman climbed out and adjusted her jacket and waved, Sulis knew with a cold certainty that this was one more person that she would never meet again. She should be used to it. Her life was full of strangers, coming, staying till she almost knew them, and then going. But as she waved back this time an odd emptiness opened inside her.

When Alison had gone there was silence in the car. Then Simon leaned forward and turned the CD on. Some jazzy music burst from the dashboard. He turned it down. 'So. Let's go.' He turned and looked at her over the back of the seat, and his face was suntanned as if from some recent holiday. 'And from now on our daughter is back from school and we're all one happy family.'

She smiled, faintly. 'Won't people ask . . .'

'We've only been here ourselves for a few months. No one knows us much. We're all new in the city.'

As she sat back, and felt the engine start, she wished he had said something else. Something more comforting. Something that welcomed her, that showed he knew she might be feeling scared, or apprehensive. But he had already turned round and was pointing out a traffic cone the car had to avoid.

Hannah drove. She chatted too, but Sulis barely heard. Because they had turned out of the car park and were passing through the streets, and the buildings rose on each side of her now in stately beauty, their Georgian facades calm and orderly, their names carved, their door frames of white wood, the railings around their sunken areas painted black and hung with window boxes and baskets of flowers.

As the car droned up behind a red double-decker bus full of tourists, Sulis hugged the purple rucksack to her chest and tried not to smile too broadly. She had seen photographs, but they had not done the city justice. The sun was out and the golden streets were brilliant with shoppers, cars and crowds of visitors. Gulls and starlings flapped on the housetops. At the top of the road the car turned left then right into a street of grand proportions, the houses in a stately row, their high windows shining. She felt as if they were courtiers, lined up on each side to escort her up the hill, beautiful old buildings that filled her with a sense of calm, the perfect orderliness of the city. And as the car turned the last corner she gave a gasp of surprise, and Hannah grinned at her in the driving mirror. 'Great, isn't it? It always gets me too.'

They had entered a circle of houses. Three streets led to it like the spokes of a wheel. As the car purred slowly round Sulis felt a sort of quiet delight. The facade of the circle held her inside it, it rose to the blue sky. Pillared, with three storeys of white tall windows, the houses were not separate, they were all one terrace, and along the roofline huge stone acorns stood at regular intervals.

The pavements were broad, the railings black and glossy. In the heart of the encircled space five huge trees soared well above the rooftops.

'Welcome to the King's Circus,' Simon said.

'You live *here*?'

He nodded. 'Not a whole house, that would cost a fortune. But we've got an apartment, on the top floor. Great views.'

Hannah pulled into the kerb. 'This is it, Sulis.'

As she climbed out and stood on the pavement, Sulis had the strangest feeling that she had somehow come home, though she had never, as far as she remembered, been here before. Since that terrible day when she was seven she had lived in a dozen different flats and houses, some of them poky, most of them average, once even on a farm out on the Yorkshire moors. But never anything like this. The step, the white door with its gilt knocker, the airy hallway floored in black and white tiles, the staircase curving upwards, were all beautiful. She let Simon bring the bags; she was too eager to run up behind Hannah and see.

'There's a Mr Thomas in the basement – businessman,' Hannah called back, her small hands sliding up the wooden rail. 'Mrs Wilson on the first – ancient, been here years and years. Couple on the second. Second-homers, from London, I think. Only here weekends. And then there's us.'

She threaded the key in the lock, and opened the

door. 'Your room's in the attic. I'd better go down and give him a hand. His back's a bit dodgy, though he'll never admit it.'

She clattered down.

Sulis dropped her bag on a chair. She wandered into a high space of perfect whiteness, gauzy curtains at its lofty windows. A leather sofa with books dumped on it, a table, a TV, music. A faint smell of candle smoke. Beyond was a corridor with doors off, and at the end, tiny and white, a wooden stair. She ran up it, and found a bathroom and a narrow passageway that must have been designed for servants. It led to a small scratched door.

'Found it?' Simon called up the stairs.

'Yes,' she said.

'Great. Tea or coffee?'

'Tea. Please.' She stood in the opened doorway. A long, low room, white panelled walls, white-painted floorboards. A rug, a desk, a chair, a bed. The only big thing here was the window, a great flat rectangle of glass, and she opened it and found to her delight that she could step out, that there was a platform behind the stonework balustrade. A gull flapped off, complaining. Sulis ducked through the window and pulled herself upright, one arm gripped tightly round the pedestal of one of the great acorns. The stone was hot under her hands. Before her the King's Circus stood in its perfection, as if it focused on her like some polite, remote audience.

Cars circled dizzily at her feet, a woman with a pushchair walked the pavement, and in the trees a crowd of jackdaws rose and cawed and settled.

She stood there in the sky wondering why she felt so scared. As if delight could terrify you. And she wondered what sort of person this new life would make her.

Who this Sulis would turn out to be.

Zac

Two men were lighting the lamps in the street outside a dingy tavern. When I asked them the way they stared like the fools they were.

'You'm from the North, mazter?'

'None of your business.'

They grinned at each other. Probably at my accent. One said, 'The new house is thataway, in Giles Alley she be.'

'Thank you.' As I walked away I felt their eyes on my back, & I gripped the handle of the sword-stick Forrest had told me to carry. The city, he had said, was dangerous at night. A low snigger of laughter told me they were still watching. One of them called out. 'Be careful going in that house, zurr. There be a ghost in she.'

The lower classes in this place talk in a soft, furry dialect, all aars & urrs. It's taken me weeks to understand a word they say. I splashed through the filthy runnels of the street, stepped over a pile of muck & turned into what must be Giles Alley.

It was pitch black. The houses leaned together overhead & blocked out the sky with their decrepit eaves. Something like a rat ran over my boot; I stabbed at it, but it streaked into a hole. As I walked on, my footsteps rang in the narrow slot. Was this really the place?

I stopped. It struck me that those men might have sent me down here for some jest or darker purpose. Robbery. Even murder! My fingers tightened on the sweaty grip of the sword-stick. I looked back.

The night stank of decayed vegetables & ordure. In this quarter Aquae Sulis was still a fetid warren of dark alleys, & for a moment I could see why my new master Forrest raged so about it, & how his vision of a city made glorious with sunlit terraces & wide streets obsessed him. But no one was coming to cut my throat, so I groped onward, my gloves smeared by the slimy wall. After a while I came to an archway with a burnt-out lamp beside it, still smoking, as if it had recently been extinguished. There was no bell to jangle yet, & no gate either, so I ducked through, & found a courtyard. Dimly I could see piled heaps of building stone, & the choking dust made me sneeze, far too loudly.

The sound echoed. Above the half-finished roof the moon hung, a perfect crescent.

I wiped my eyes with a kerchief & said, 'Master Forrest? Are you here, sir?' The letter crinkled in the pocket of my waistcoat. 'It's Zac, sir.'

Of course he wasn't here. The site was deserted & the workmen gone home. Even the night-watchman was in some ginhouse.

I turned, disgusted.

Then, in the window beside me, something knocked.

I confess I froze in fear. Because there was nothing there but a dark sash casement, showing me a ghostly reflection of myself, & above the window in the stonework a half-finished carving of a crowned man, his face an obvious copy of Forrest's own. *Bladud*. The ancient druid king. My master's craziest obsession.

After a moment I crossed to the window & put my face to it, looking in, blocking out moonlight with my hands. 'Master! A message has come for you. The man said it requires an urgent answer.'

The room beyond was utterly dark. This was one of the houses Peter Bull's team were building to Forrest's design, & Bull's men were lazy. The work was weeks behind, & yesterday Forrest had stormed around the workshop in fury because he had discovered they had mixed bad stone with the good, & it would crumble to pieces in a few years.

I knocked softly. 'Sir? Are you there?'

With a great crack something hit the window full in my face. I leapt back in terror, every nerve tingling, my hand snatching out the sword-blade.

Black. Black & flying, like a winged demon!

Again it came, a hard smack, but even as I cried out

19

my fear ebbed into relief because I'd seen its eye, tiny &
bright & wild & suddenly I understood. There was a bird
trapped in the room.

I breathed out. This place was getting to me. I
straightened my shoulders & put on my most confident
air. Then I walked along to where the front door should
be & peered through the gap into the hallway. The half-
built house was a patchwork of shadows & bright spills
of moonlight; there were panels missing in the inner walls
& floorboards gaped like black traps for the unwary.

I thought about just going away. But I knew if I did
that bird would flap all night inside my dreams, & I found
it hard enough to sleep already. It would be a matter of
minutes to get the thing out.

Probing with the sword-stick I edged warily inside,
through a darkness thick with sawdust & the acrid smells
of pine & fresh turpentine. Curled shavings of wood
crunched under my heel.

As far as I could see, the hallway had three doors;
beyond them the skeleton of a staircase led up into the
gloom. I put my ear against the first door & listened.

Thumps. Rustles. A silence that lasted so long I thought
the bird must be dead. Then a harsh screech.

I turned the handle & looked in.

This room was almost finished. The panelling was
dark oak. A great marble fireplace yawned in the far wall
– that was how the bird must have got in.

I couldn't see it, but suddenly it zigzagged out of the

dark & the smack against the window glass was so vicious I knew it would break its neck in frustration if I didn't do something quickly.

I slid into the room.

Behind me, the door shut with a click.

I swore, groping desperately behind my back for the handle, but there wasn't one, & at once a slash of feathers whistled past my ear, so close I felt the draught of it. I ducked, caught with the sudden horror of the hateful bird hitting me, tangling in panic in my hair, pecking at my eyes. I dived on to hands and knees, dropping the sword-stick, cursing Peter Bull & his bone-idle workers. How could I get out with no handle on the door! Would I be stuck in here all night? Forrest was probably arriving home about now & shouting my name, & Mrs Hall was coming out of the kitchen to tell him there had been a message & that I'd gone off with it to Giles Alley. Maybe he'd come to find me.

Another swoop. There it was! It had perched on the mantelshelf, a small hunched shadow. Soft scratchings & flutterings came out of the dark. A bright eye caught moonlight. It was watching me.

Knowing where it was helped me regain my courage; I picked myself up &, keeping my gaze on it, backed towards the window.

Crack!

Shadows zigzagged all over me; I was slashed with clots of darkness.

The room was full of birds. I yelled & threw myself down. How many were there & where were they coming from? I was trapped with corpsebirds & gallowspickers! Maybe my eyeless body would be all that would be found here in the morning. At least it would scare Peter Bull witless.

I rubbed my face with a gritty hand & told myself not to be a fool. All I had to do was get to the window & throw it open & the things would fly out. Then I could climb over the sill. It was a stupid situation to be in, but no one would ever know & tomorrow I could even be witty about it.

Carefully, keeping my head low, I crawled over the rough boards. Nails stabbed my palms. Oak creaked under my sore knees. I could see the mess the birds had made now; streaks of white spattered down the oak panels, & clotted in the hearth. Jackdaws, they seemed, & all at once a sliver of moonlight came from behind a cloud, & I saw them, perched on the mantelshelf, a dark row, & may be some up on the top of the window! And one on a chair in the corner. I dared not breathe. I was almost there.

Then to my horror I put my fingers down & touched a warm hand.

I yelled! The birds erupted in panic, hitting walls, glass, smashing their frail bones. Something brushed my shoulder; I glimpsed a pale flicker of movement that made me jump up & fling myself at the window, heaving its weight upwards.

It wouldn't move. I swore & tugged again but the sill was slimy with bird muck. A black wing smacked into the glass. Feathers burst, inches from my face. I raised the stick & jabbed the blade under the sash. Sweat was blinding me. The birds, a rain of nightmare suicides, dived against the glass.

Wood splintered. I forced, harder. Behind me the door slammed open.

'*Leave that window alone, sir!*'

The voice was calm & it froze me like a douche of cold water.

Forrest stood in the doorway, staring at the black birds that swooped around him. He strode across the room, pushed me aside, & hauled the new ill-fitting sash upwards with both hands, so that a gust of rainy air burst in, scattering us both with drizzle.

I staggered up. Even now I ached to keep my arm across my eyes, but not in front of him.

'Stand aside,' he snapped. 'Give them space.'

Three birds swooped out. Another hit the chimney with a crunch that made me wince.

Forrest clapped his hands, moved in, waved gently. The last bird fluttered. It circled us & landed, gripping with clumsy talons, on the back of the chair. Forrest's shadow was huge on the wall.

'Go on now,' he said, reaching out to it. 'Fly free, dark spirit.'

But the jackdaw didn't go. Instead it hopped on to his hand.

Was he as astonished as I? It was the most extraordinary thing. The bird & my master regarded each other, beady black eye to calm brown, as if some silent message passed between them. I saw the scaly claws dig into Forrest's skin, the glossy feathered body adjusting its balance.

A second of stillness.

Then it flapped & was gone, out into the rainy night.

'Amazing!' I breathed.

Forrest nodded, slowly. 'A truly druidical moment.' He seemed to remain for an instant in that magic. Then he breathed out & glanced at me, & I saw the folly of the situation swim back into his eyes. 'Zac, what in God's name have you done to yourself?'

I was suddenly aware of dust & filth smeared on my hands and face. And my clothes! Ruined!

'I was looking for you, sir. Then I realized . . . the birds were trapped.'

'What a mess!' Forrest strode to the hearth & bent under it, looking up. 'That lackwit Peter Bull hasn't capped the chimney. I swear that man will put me in my grave . . .'

I said quietly, 'Sir. There is someone else in the room.'

He turned. In the moonlight I saw his fine face, & his eyes, with their steady gaze that often unnerved me. Then he saw where I was pointing.

She was crouched in the corner, behind the chair. Something grey & sack-like was pulled about her, & she huddled there under it as if even now she thought she was hidden from us. Just for a moment I almost thought her a ghost indeed, she was so pale & thin.

Forrest surprised me. He crouched down, & his voice was very soft, as it had been with the bird. 'Who are you?'

She made a small sound. Between a sob & a murmur.

Forrest looked up. 'Get a light, Zac. Quick now.'

As I went out I heard her speak. She said, 'Sylvia.'

It took me a while to find a tinderbox & lantern in the foreman's office, & when I brought it back to the room the girl was sitting on the chair & Forrest was standing by the fireplace. I had the feeling he had moved away from her as he heard me come. I placed the lantern carefully on the rough floorboards. Then I stared at the girl.

She was very pretty.

But her face was thin & dirty & pocked with raw pustules that she scratched at, constantly. Her hair was coppery red, a rich colour, & it had been pinned up, but now it was all coming down on her shoulders. She clutched the grey cloak around her, but I could see a shoe, almost a slipper, on her left foot, of white silk embroidered with tiny flowers. Hardly outdoor footwear.

She was talking quickly, gabbling & breathless with sobs, but I could see at once that she trusted him.

He said, 'Surely you cannot be forced to . . .'

'Sir, you are respectable, you don't know these people. I can't go back, sir, I can't! Please don't make me go back there!'

So she'd run away. And I had a shrewd idea from where. The city reeks with gambling dens & houses of improper women. She smelt too, of sweat & pomade. And surely, drink.

Jonathan Forrest watched her intently. His great shadow & mine & hers flickered together on the wall. Forrest wore his usual fustian coat of brown & a waistcoat in the same dull shade. He makes no effort with his clothes. His boots were cracked & muddy, & unlike my father, or any other gentleman I know, he rarely bothers with a wig. But then he's the son of a builder, & hardly a gentleman . . .

'Where is this place?' he asked.

She hung her head. 'They call it Gibson's, sir. Down near the baths.'

'And they make you . . .'

'They make me draw the rich young gentlemen in. By talk & . . . suchlike. So that they gamble & drink & lose all their money. As I have lost mine. And if I stay there I fear what else will happen to me.'

'Have you fled tonight?'

'I have, sir.'

'Where will you go?'

She shrugged. I glimpsed a blue satin dress of sleazy

finery cut low, but she grabbed at the cloak & drew it tighter. 'My family live in a village up on the downs, but they won't want me. Not now. I would be a disgrace to them. I was thinking I might travel to London . . .'

'London!' Forrest sounded appalled. 'Girl, London is a hell of vices! You wouldn't last a week.'

'Then Bristol, sir. Anywhere. If I had some money, I could find a lodging. Honest work.'

So there it was, the begging. He would give her a few coins, I was sure. He was a soft touch & even beggars in the street could see him coming.

He turned & stared at the white-streaked fireplace as if he was thinking so deeply he didn't even see it, & in that instant the girl darted a look at me. A slant of blue eyes, & then they were fixed back on him. But enough to see she didn't like me at all.

'Zac. Lock the window & make sure the house is secure.' He turned, held out a hand to the girl & raised her up. 'You, Miss Sylvia, are coming home with me.'

I thought I had misheard him.

She too stared. She said, 'Sir, I don't think . . .'

'You will be able to bathe, & my housekeeper will feed you & find you clothes that are more suitable. There's a room in the servants' attics you can sleep in. Tomorrow, we can decide your future.'

I don't know when I've felt a greater disgust. I couldn't help bursting out, 'Sir . . . your standing in the city . . .'

He looked at me so hard my words dried. Then he

turned back to her. 'I mean no harm to you, Sylvia, & you need have no fears about me. You understand me?'

'I . . . I'm sure, sir, but . . .' She shook her head. 'It wouldn't be right.'

She just wanted money. I was sure of it now. I wondered if her story was even true.

'Come on.' He waved her towards the door.

Then he came back, quickly, to where I stood. 'I forgot. This letter. Where is it?'

I took it out & gave it to him, & as soon as he saw the seal he gave a great gasp of delight & strode swiftly away with the lantern, leaving the girl & I in the dark. As we watched him open the paper she said quietly, 'And who are you, Master Peacock?'

I stared at her. Because the self-pity had vanished from her voice & for a moment a quirky, quizzical amusement flickered in her face. I remembered that she had seen my panic among the birds.

Then Forrest gave a great cry. 'At last!'

'Sir?' I stepped towards him, but instantly he crushed the letter into his pocket & hurried to the door. 'Do what I said, Zac. Secure the place.' He was flushed with sudden joy, that air of craziness that sometimes overtakes him. They were both gone before I could say more.

In the dark I closed the window, jammed the catch & took a brief look round the house, but my thoughts were not on it. Instead I was sunk in gloom. What a fortune was mine, to be the son of a rich man so crushed by debt that I must be apprenticed to this lunatik who lived in dreams of building a perfect city, & yet could not recognize a harlot when he saw one.

As I walked home through the squalid alleys, I brooded on just how bad his taking her in would look. Because she would end up staying. I could foresee that. Just like the dog he had brought home, & the three cats that shed their fur everywhere in the house.

How could I live in such a household?

I am not self-righteous. I am as much a rake as any man. But I do not bring it home with me.

By the time I turned into Queen Square I was thoroughly ruffled, & yet the sight of the tall, elegant houses, their harmony and perfection in the moonlight, calmed my nerves. Queen's Square was Forrest's best work yet. He could get some things right. Perhaps I should see his actions as the eccentricities of a genius; after all, everyone knew all such men were mad.

I let myself in & went to climb the stairs, but as I passed the workroom I saw his coat, flung on the back of a chair.

I stopped. His voice & Mrs Hall the housekeeper's argued upstairs.

Glancing round, I stepped across quickly & thrust my fingers in the pocket. The thick paper of the letter crackled as I unfolded it.

I stared at it, astonished.

No letter at all, but a drawing. It was a two-faced

image, a Janus, one face staring back, one forwards. One male, the other female. And all around it, in a great circle, so that its own tail rested in its own mouth, was a narrow serpent.

Below, someone had written a single word in spiky writing.

OROBOROS.

I had no idea what it meant.

Bladud

*I dreamed of the family I had left behind. I wandered
oakwoods and the bare downs, and the raven-wind screamed
in my ears as I lay deep under the leaves.*

*You out there in your warm house, how can you know how a
lost soul feels?*

*My disease erupted in pools and quagmires, ran in the rivers
like fever. I was the land and it was a winter world. Disease
comes in many forms. It can be obsession, it can be mania.
A man can spread it even to his friends.*

*One day demons came out of the oakwoods to torment me.
They grunted and snuffled. They had great snouts and their
bodies were pale as fungi.*

*At right they lay down around me, earthpigs and boars and
beasts of legend. I became one of them, following their trails,
eating the mast and mushrooms they dug out.*

They fought and roared and laughed at me.

*And I began to see how often they roamed deep into the
heartwood of a remote valley, and always when they came*

back the scabs of their pocked skin had cleared to a
clean health.

Hope is such a frail thing. Such a tiny glimmer in
the darkness.

I was worn thin and exhausted. Maybe that was why the
thought took so long to come.

It formed slowly in my mind like the light in the east before
dawn.

It said to me, 'If you go where the demons go, will you be
cured too?'

I followed them.

For dark days I crawled like a beast down and down into the
marshy valley.

Steams rose around me. Tiny insects whined and bit me.

I put my paw and snout to the ground and splashed in water
that was hot.

I crawled inside the circle of its comfort.

Sulis

She had unpacked everything except the blue file.

It lay at the bottom of her bag, in the secret zipped compartment. For a moment she gazed at it, as she sat cross-legged on the bed in her pyjamas, with the sunlight coming almost horizontally through the open window. Jackdaws karked in the trees of the Circus.

Then she unzipped the pocket and took the file out.

Why did she keep it? In all the moves, the different bedrooms, the endless foster-homes, the file had come with her. If this was a new life, she should get rid of it.

Instead she opened it, took out the photocopies of the newspaper cuttings, and spread them on the duvet.

They were grubby now, and split where she had kept them folded for so long. No one knew she had them. Twelve cuttings, all from different newspapers, and they had all used the same photograph. The famous, only photograph anyone had ever managed to get. A small, startled child of seven, caught getting out of a car, her

33

red hair in frizzy curls, her wide eyes dazzled by the flash of the camera, her hand tight in a policewoman's. She wore a striped hooded top and little-girl trousers with pink flowers on them. She was so small, so skinny. Above her the headlines screamed.

CHILD DEATH MYSTERY
WHAT HAS SHE SEEN?
TERROR IN THE PLAYGROUND

Sulis lifted one of the pages and brought the photo up close to her eyes so that the image became a blur of ink. Then, equally slowly, she drew it back down into focus. Either way it was the same. The girl in the photograph wasn't her any more.

The car had probably been an unmarked police car. There had been many and she couldn't remember this one, but she remembered the camera. It had been thrust in her face, and the flash had terrified her, and the policewoman – that had been Jean – had gone berserk and tried to grab the man, and he'd got away on a motorbike.

He must have made a fortune from the photograph.

She raised her head and looked in the wavy mirror Hannah had bought for her wall. She saw a different girl from the one on the photo. A thinner, tighter face. A blue, steady gaze that gave nothing away. Her hair was dyed blonde now and hung straight to her shoulders

– she looked like thousands of other girls of her age. Average height, average weight. Her clothes were without personality. She'd chosen them carefully, avoiding sparkle, bright colour, too much flesh. No images, no slogans. She looked like a student – any student. That was the disguise. That was Sulis.

After a moment she folded the papers and pushed them back into the zipped compartment. She shoved the bag to the back of the wardrobe, shut the door, locked it, and put the little key in her pocket. Hannah and Simon were very keen to give her privacy. That made a change.

She said to her reflection, 'New face, new house, new life. All you need now is some money.'

Downstairs, at breakfast in the small kitchen hung with herbs, she licked yoghurt from her spoon and said quietly, 'I'd like to get a job, if you don't mind. Do my bit towards the housekeeping.'

Her new parents looked at each other. Hannah poured skimmed milk on to her home-made muesli. Carefully she said, 'Sulis, that's very kind, but we have to think about your safety. This is a city full of tourists – they come from all over, including the North. Someone might recognize you . . .'

'They won't. Ten years is a long time. I don't even recognize me any more.'

'It may seem a long time at your age.' Simon had put the newpaper down. 'For some of us it's barely yesterday.

Besides, if it's about money, there's really no need. We both work.' He glanced at Hannah anxiously. 'And, well social services pay towards your upkeep.'

Sulis nodded. 'I don't mind.'

'Mind?'

'That they pay you to look after me. I didn't expect you to do it for free.'

Was that harsh? They were so easy to surprise. They were different from the couples she had been with before. So wide-open, so idealistic. She could see Simon now, caught in awkwardness, as if he was listening to the soft classical music from the radio, but really her words had stung him. She should be careful. He was already a bit wary of her.

So she said, 'It's not just about money. In October I start uni. I have to get used to going out, being around people. I have to start building my own life. That's the whole point of coming here. Once I'm eighteen I'm on my own, and I have to be ready.'

Hannah came and sat at the table. 'Are you sure you can face it?'

'I'm not scared.'

'What sort of job?'

Sulis put the spoon in the dish. 'Waitress? Something in a shop? It need only be till term starts . . . something quiet. There must be loads of holiday work here. As you said, it's full of tourists.'

Hannah looked at Simon. For a moment only the

piano music filled the kitchen, and the drone of a car outside.

'We'll have to check with ... the authorities,' Simon said.

Sulis shrugged.

'Well look.' Hannah folded her fingers. 'If they agree I have a friend who works down at the baths. She goes to my yoga class. She was telling me yesterday that one of their summer girls had left them in the lurch a bit. I could find out ...'

'Baths?' Sulis stared. 'You mean as some sort of lifeguard?'

There was a split second of embarrassment. Then Simon said, 'No,' and Hannah laughed nervously. 'No, I mean the Roman baths, Sulis. The museum. The hot spring.'

'Oh. Right.'

'The Waters of Sulis.' Simon folded his paper, went over to the door and stopped, halfway through it. Behind him in the huge white sitting room she could see his drawing board in the window, the long gauzy curtains drifting over it. 'It will depend on Alison.'

'Fine.' Sulis raised her eyes and stared at him, for just a second too long. Then she smiled.

'We wouldn't want them to feel left out, would we?'

In fact, she thought later, listening to Hannah making

calls, it didn't matter what Alison or anyone else thought. They'd ruled her life for years but she was going to be free of them now. She was in her ideal city now.

The sitting-room windows looked down on the Circus.

At this time in the morning it was fairly quiet. A few pedestrians walked by, a man sat with a newspaper on the solitary bench, a white van with *Peter Bull Builders* on drove slowly round. The leaves of the central trees were still green, with only one or two shading to early russet.

In the morning sun the perfect curving facade of the houses was a satisfaction to her. She could never tire of looking at it. It was a circle of gold and she was safe inside it. Then she noticed there were carvings, a row of emblems all the way round, above the doorways. She leaned closer, trying to see them more clearly. Why hadn't she noticed them before?

From the hall, Hannah's voice drifted through opera from the radio. 'Oh yes . . . fine. That sounds really the best thing. Ruth, it's so kind of you . . . Oh the flat is wonderful thanks . . .'

Sulis smiled to herself. Why had she chosen Simon and Hannah? She could have gone abroad – there were people in France who'd offered to take her. France would really have been a new life.

But she knew why. It was because of the city.

Simon came in and took a book out of the shelves. One whole wall of the room was lined with them, big expensive books on architecture and art. She said, 'Who designed this street?'

He came up and gazed out, reflected in the glass panes. 'The Circus? A man called Jonathan Forrest. A brilliant, crazy man. Obsessed with druids and magic. He was one of the first to survey Stonehenge – properly, I mean, not just some higgledy-piggledy drawing. They say he based the design of the Circus on various stone circles. There are thirty houses in the Circus, and thirty stones in the outer circle of Stonehenge. The dimensions are exactly the same as the Great Ring at Stanton Drew, not far from here. He went there and measured the place in a hailstorm. Some people say this whole street is a magical construct.'

Was that why she felt at home here? She said, 'It must be a great place for an architect to live. Every time you look out, there it is.'

'Bye!' Hannah said, laughing, into the phone. 'See you Friday!'

Simon nodded. 'Spaces are important – the shapes of them. Where they are on the earth. I think there's something about this place that you can never quite get at. You keep thinking you know what it's about, but it curves away from you, and all of a sudden it's coming up behind you, surprising you. Like a secret.'

Catching her eyes on him in the glass he stopped. 'Sorry. I didn't mean . . .'

'It's OK,' she said quietly.

Hannah came in, her pretty face alight. 'Well, Sulis, if you really want the job it's there. Some girl has gone off to Lanzarote without telling anyone, and Ruth's desperate. She says can you go down this afternoon for a chat. I can come with you . . .'

'No,' she said. 'Thanks, but I can go on my own.'

Hannah glanced at Simon. 'Are we doing the right thing?'

'I think so, angel.'

Sulis watched him kiss Hannah's cheek and go out. Their affection fascinated her.

She said, 'What do they pay me?'

Hannah looked confused; she pushed back the tangle of hair from her eyes. 'Oh, do you know, I forgot to ask! Shall I ring back . . . ?'

'No.' Sulis shook her head, and managed a rueful smile. 'I'll find out.'

For a moment, then, she had felt older than Hannah, as if Hannah was some ditzy, hopeless little sister.

And maybe she *was* older, because Hannah had never lived in terror for her life. Hannah had never lain awake at night wondering if *he* was out there. If *he* was still looking for her.

It was raining when she walked down the steps into the Circus, and that was good, because she could put an umbrella up and keep it low over her face. The wide pavement gleamed in the downpour; the black railings were speckled with fat raindrops. She walked round and down the hill, seeing the city's glorious splendour below her.

She'd always loved buildings. Other kids had played with dolls and guns, but even in nursery she had only played with the bricks. A set of yellow and green and blue wooden blocks. That must have been how she'd met Caitlin, because Caitlin had liked to play with them too.

She walked quickly, through parked cars, dodging the traffic. The city was busy, its shops full of people. She passed the banks and some boutiques, hearing a few American accents. Above the rooftops the sky was blue and yet cloud boiled up there; a gusty shower spattered the umbrella.

She and Caitlin had spent hours playing with the bricks. Towers mostly, that fell when some kid jarred the table, or houses with yellow walls and blue doors and a red roof. She had never been able to get a chimney on them; she half smiled now, remembering how annoying that had been. And Caitlin had helped, chattering on like little kids do. It had only taken days for them to become best friends.

At the bottom of the hill the road changed. The beautiful, measured symmetry of the shops disappeared; the streets became smaller and less regular; she took a right turn and found herself in a network of narrow alleys and steps leading down, as if this part of

41

town was left over from some older tangle, before Jonathan Forrest and those like him imposed order, and harmony.

Under the dripping umbrella she felt she was suddenly being led into her fractured past, that time when she was small and the world a place of exaggerated hugeness – high steps, big chairs, conversations of adults as meaningless as the leaves that rustled high above her head. Best not to think of it. Nor of Caitlin.

Too late. Already the old anxiety had come back and she turned, circling to glance behind her. Shoppers.

Kids, running.

A man.

He was far back, right up at the top of the narrow alley. He was gazing into a shop window, a man in a dark raincoat, his face turned away from her, and she stared at him hard, because all at once she was afraid that he might have been the man reading a newspaper on the bench in the Circus that morning.

No.

Yes.

She didn't know.

She turned, took a deep breath and told herself to stop imagining things. No one knew where she was. She was safe.

She made herself walk slow, and steady. Rain had turned the pavements glossy; colours from the windows ran and splashed under her feet like paint on a wet canvas. Down a few steps on the right a shop doorway opened; a dark interior of hanging mobiles, wind chimes, cases of silver jewellery. She ducked inside, closed the umbrella and stood with her back to the doorway, watching its dim outline in a mirror on the wall.

After a minute, the man passed.

He wore a cap now, pulled down in the rain, and his coat was long. A newspaper was bundled under his arm. She caught a glimpse of a sharp face, dark hair. He didn't look to the side.

She drifted round the shop, gazing unseeing at rows of silver rings.

Lots of people carried newspapers. It meant nothing.

She hung around for ten minutes, then said, 'Thanks', to the disappointed girl behind the counter, and edged out.

The rain had stopped. Watery sunlight broke over the houses.

She ran, quickly, down to the Abbey churchyard.

As she had expected, it was full of tourists. They stood around watching the jugglers that busked here, taking photos and roaring with laughter at the comedy routine. Sulis edged past a queue of Japanese schoolchildren outside the museum; she had to push through and she stumbled suddenly out into an open space at the front.

She bumped into a pig.

It was huge, and plastic. Pink flowers had been

painted all over it, and grass on its hooves and legs. In its snout a great ring gleamed.

'Ticket please.'

The boy was about her age, wearing a shirt and a badge saying 'SECURITY'.

Sulis said, 'I haven't got one. I'm looking for Mrs Ruth Matthews. About the job.'

'Oh.' He glanced behind her at the impatient schoolkids. 'Well you'd better ask at the desk. They'll get her.'

At that moment the doors opened and the schoolkids flooded in like a great tide. She was shoved against the boy and they both lurched into the pig. It wobbled and she grabbed at it, and so did he. She said, 'Why on earth is this here?'

'Part of an installation,' the boy said shortly. 'Some artist's done it. Pigs. All colours. All over the city.'

He pulled a face, and she giggled. Then her face froze.

Behind the kids, just for a second, she saw the pavement cafe outside, a man sipping coffee, staring straight at her through the chattering crowd.

'All right?' the boy asked.

She nodded. Numb.

Zac

I was daydreaming in the workroom when I heard them arrive. Glancing down, I saw I'd drawn the serpent eating its tail on the side of the plan I was supposed to be completing. I slid a paper over it quickly. Then I went to the door & opened it. Just a crack.

There were three visitors. One I knew at once; Ralph Alleyn, who owned the stone quarries on the downs above the town. He & Forrest were friends – Forrest had even designed a house for him – I had seen it, a grandiose, florid extravagance too big for its space. Alleyn was a tall man, easy in his wealth, his suit an elegant blue damask. He came in talking & laughing, his aquiline face and powdered wig contrasting with my master's darkness. Forrest shook his hand with unusual warmth.

'Good to see you, Ralph.'

'You too, old magus. Are you ready for them?'

'I am. But I fear my strange plan may scare them off.'

Alleyn laughed. He said nothing else.

The other two I didn't know, but I guessed them to be councillors, & therefore Forrest's enemies. Was he reduced to asking them for money? He showed them in, very formally, then turned too quickly & caught my eye at the crack of the door. I jumped back, but he snapped, 'Zac! Come in here & take notes of this.'

I caught up pen & paper & hurried after him. Forrest's study is a narrow, book-lined room. He has a great plan table in the centre of it, where he designs & writes his lunatik books, & a few chairs, the upholstery worn & stained from ink. He usually works standing, or paces in restless energy up & down on the threadbare rug.

The best thing about the room is the ceiling, which I like because it has a great skylight. Today it let in a warm shaft of autumn light that I went & sat in, on a stool in the corner. The visitors gave me cold stares, so I rose & bowed. Forrest said, 'Master Zachariah Stoke. My assistant.'

'He'll be staying?'

'He'll be taking notes. If you don't object.'

The small fat sweaty one shrugged. 'If you insist.'

'Ralph,' Forrest said. 'May I present the Honourable Thomas Greye.'

Alleyn bowed to the fat man. 'Master Greye is an old acquaintance.'

Forrest nodded. He turned. The other man was younger, in fact not much older than me, disgustingly handsome & spectacularly well-dressed. I ground my teeth as I saw the cut of his suit, the soft Spanish leather of his boots.

'And this is Lord Compton.'

Ralph looked surprised. 'Indeed? But I had thought Lord Compton was . . . forgive me . . . an elderly man.'

'My uncle died in Rome, last year.' The boy chose the best chair & sat in it, legs spread. Idly he tapped the heap of brown-backed books with his cane, sending a few of them sliding. 'I inherited his whole fortune. I intend to double it as soon as possible.'

Forrest's voice was flat & sardonic. 'Well this city is the place to make money. If money is what you want.' His disapproval was obvious to me. But Lord Compton merely placed his cane on the table & leaned back, smiling. Already I wanted to punch him.

'The place is so crowded. With these crowds of visitors it's becoming a bearpit.' Thomas Greye flicked dust from a chair & sat. 'Fops & queans & card-sharps, that's what this city attracts. Pick-pockets, gamblers, whores. We're a honeypot for the buzzing vermin of England.'

Ralph Alleyn laughed. 'Perhaps. But they come to prey on the rich who flock to our healing waters. And rich men need fine houses, gentlemen. We will provide them. Superb streets, squares fit for kings. John's designs are our fortune.'

I wrote that down scornfully. Up on the wall, the portrait of Forrest's wife, dead these ten years, watched me suspiciously.

The fat man, Greye, was the talker. He had a ring on every chubby finger & they were all gold & one of them would have halved my father's debts. He said, 'Houses, yes. Queen's Square has been a great success, I will grant you. So what plan have you for the high field? I have heard rumours . . .'

'Let me show you,' Forrest said quickly. I heard the tension in his voice & knew he couldn't wait any longer. Last night he had not slept well, wheezing with his asthma. There was still a breathlessness in his voice.

Ralph came eagerly to the table, which was covered with a white cloth. Under it something tall & lumpy waited. As Forrest reached out to it, Lord Compton's drawl cut across the room.

'You presume to design for gentlemen, sir.' His head turned. His eyes were blue and very steady. 'And yet it's common talk in the city that you yourself keep a, shall we say, immoral girl in your house. I am shocked, sir.'

My pen stopped over the page.

I glanced up.

Forrest had his back to them but was facing me. He has dark eyes, & now they seemed almost black with a flame of rage. His fingers tensed on the white cloth. He saw me staring so I glanced down, but what I thought was, *Like the serpent, he gnaws at his own skin . . .*

'My household is my own business.'

'Indeed it is,' Alleyn said quickly. 'I'm sure Lord

Compton meant nothing . . .'

'Oh no.' Compton rose, smiling coldly at Forrest's back. 'I meant nothing at all.' In the mirror he raised one eyebrow at me. I just stared back. But oddly enough, I no longer wanted to punch him. The gossip about Sylvia was all over the town. Forrest made no secret of the way she was living here. He had walked out openly with her, bought her clothes, boots, a parasol. Had he adopted her? Was she a servant? No one knew. Neither, I was sure, did he.

'The scheme, sir.' Alleyn came up behind Forrest. 'We're so anxious to see it. Aren't we, Master Greye?'

The fat man mopped his face, 'I don't give a mouldy fig how many loose women a man keeps. Business is business. Show us the scheme, man.'

Alleyn glanced at Forrest. For a moment I wondered at their friendship. They were so different; Alleyn urbane & anxious to please, my master as erratic as quicksilver, convinced of his own genius. But he held his temper now & I almost felt sorry for him. He turned to the table & swept the cloth aside as if the pleasure of the moment had suddenly gone.

'Gentlemen,' he said, moodily. 'My new scheme. I call it the King's Circus.'

It was not a plan at all, but a model, superbly made of fine woods, & at last I knew why the lamp burned for long hours of the night in his dim room.

The three men stared.

Finally Greye said,'Bless my damned soul.'

I stood up, & edged a little closer, my notes sliding to the floor.

The model was of a street, but it was not straight. *It was a circle of houses.* The continuous facade was an astonishingly beautiful design of regular columns, as if these were not individual houses for ordinary people at all, but some vast ancient temple, or the arena of a Roman emperor. The columns rose in the three styles of classical Greece, one above the other – Doric, Ionic, Corinthian. I am, I confess, a lazy student but I'd already learned these. And the daring of the design amazed me. A circle of houses! So simple. Why had no one thought of it before? Did it mean that Forrest was a genius after all?

'Pure local stone.' Forrest spoke into the shocked silence, his voice a little hoarse. 'Thirty houses, each built according to the owner's requirements, each different, but uniting them all, the facade. As we did with Queen's Square. But this time a perfect amphitheatre.'

Three roads radiated from it. The Circus's heart was a bare disc of pavement. I edged closer, fascinated, but no one noticed me. They were all staring at the model in an odd, stricken way. The silence went on a moment too long.

Alleyn broke it. He said,'Quite . . . unique.'

He wandered around the model, his pale hands touching a chimney, a roof. I sensed he was searching for the right words. 'John, it's sublime. It will be your greatest triumph.'

Watching Greye's shock & Compton's smirk, I suddenly didn't think so.

'A circular street?' Greye said.

Forrest nodded. He was pacing, unable to stand still. 'The circle. The shape of the universe. Perfect, without flaw. Seen from any point on its circumference, always the same. The image of the sun itself. And within it the equilateral triangle, symbol of the Trinity. To live here—'

'To live there, sir, would be insupportable!' Greye burst out. 'There is no prospect, sir. No view! Look out of your window & all around you the same endless facade! The very air would be trapped & stale. The dust, sir, would be unable to escape. The noisy echoes of horses & carriages would reverberate to uproar!' His small face contorted into a sneer; he waved a hand in agitation. 'How can you ask gentlemen & ladies of style to promenade in such a . . . giddy curve? There is nowhere to go but around & around, like rats in a cage!'

Forrest flushed. I sat quickly & pretended to write though I'm sure he won't read any of this rubbish. More likely throw it at my head.

'Oh surely that's too strong,' Alleyn said. 'After all, it will be above the town. Sweet airs & wholesome breezes, Greye. No noxious miasmas up there.'

His words fell into a pit of silence. Greye harrumphed. It was Lord Compton they were waiting for, of course.

The money bag. His gaze on the model was one of rather surprised fascination. He lifted his cane, & for a moment I thought he intended the structure some harm. Forrest stiffened. But all his lordship did was point, elegantly.

'I suppose this is some temple of the druids?'

I saw Ralph Alleyn wince. He and I both knew a trap when we saw it. But my master walked right into it.

'Yes. I believe their temples to have been circular.'

'And you've based the design on?'

'My survey of Stone-henge, sir. The greatest druidic temple in the land.'

'*Stone-henge?*' The word fell like an icy sneer.

Alleyn tried to intervene but it was too late. Jonathan Forrest was lost in his enthusiasm. 'Indeed! I believe that the druids had a great city once, at Aquae Sulis, before the Romans ever came to these islands. At Stanton Drew circle they had a university where they studied the stars & the workings of the universe. At Wookey Hole near Wells unknown rites were carried on. Here, at the sacred springs, wise men performed marvels of healing. They discovered the secrets of the body, its proportions & harmonies. The spaces of living. It was a great edifice of learning, sir, & its king was Bladud, a priest from beyond the North Wind.'

I wrote it all hurriedly, but faster than my hand could scribble, Forrest's obsessions poured out of him, as if a floodgate had been opened. His voice had changed; it was quick & bright & totally absorbed. He paced in agitation. 'Imagine it, gentlemen! We can recreate such places of learning & magic! We can discover what lies under these filthy alleys & scabrous gambling houses. Perhaps there are gilded palaces, a temple of the goddess. Think of our building a city of stately streets, their very shapes those of the sun & the moon! The improvements to the health of the poor, to sanitation! The Games that—'

Compton pounced, with the languorous malice of a cat. '*Games?*'

I stopped writing.

'Yes, of course. My Circus, like the Colosseum of Rome, could hold Games. The beauty of the human body engaged in . . .'

'Chariot races, perhaps?'

Forrest frowned. 'Well. I hardly think . . .'

'Gladiators?' Lord Compton's voice was rich with mockery.

'I . . .'

'Christians thrown to the lions? Ruffians wrestling naked in the mud for all the ladies to see?'

Forrest was silent. He looked round at us, slightly dazed, as if only now he saw the pit into which he had crashed. The sunlight from the casement above fell on him, & made the model of the circular street a deep well of shadow. What a lunatik he was! I felt hot & embarrassed at even being in the same room . . . I held the pen so tight my hand ached.

'I think what John means,' Alleyn said nervously, 'is . . .'

'What he means only God knows.' Compton eyed the model arrogantly. 'But a circular building is madness. Anyone can see that. I won't be investing my money in it, & I suggest to you, Master Alleyn, that you sell your stone to someone who'll build a decent terrace.'

He turned as if to go.

And at that moment the door opened.

Now Forrest always has a cup of chocolate about this time each morning, & whether Cook had forgotten there were visitors I don't know, but when he turned furiously to bark at the maid for interrupting it wasn't the maid at all . . . It was Sylvia.

She stood in the doorway holding the tray with the silver chocolate pot in her hands, frozen, as if in terror. The men all stared at her.

She wore an oyster silk dress Forrest had insisted on buying for her. It was ridiculously expensive & yet it suited her. She was clean & her red hair was arranged neatly, but now her face was nearly as flushed. For a moment I thought she'd drop the tray.

I jumped up, just as Forrest snapped, 'Zac.'

I took the tray from her; she let go quickly, bobbed the speediest of curtseys & would have fled but Lord Compton said, 'So this is the young . . . woman.'

He edged me aside with his cane & stared at her. 'Very pretty.'

54

His gaze was appraising & bold. Not like you'd look at a lady. Sylvia held his eye a frightened instant, & the thought came to me like a flash of light from nowhere. She knows him.

Then she looked deliberately away from both of us to Forrest. 'I'm sorry for interrupting, sir,' she said. 'I didn't know . . .'

'That's all right. Thank you, Sylvia.'

Her dress rustled as she turned; she caught at it as if to keep it quiet. Ralph Alleyn held the door for her. She might not be a lady but he was certainly a gentleman.

I cleared some papers & dumped the tray on the workbench but when I looked up something had changed in the room, as if the girl had left more than her faint rose perfume behind in the air.

Then Greye said, 'Well, I'll have to give this some thought.' He looked at Compton. 'Are you coming, sir?'

His lordship was staring at the closed door, & I didn't like his face. Then he tapped his boot with the cane & looked up, hard, at Forrest. 'I'll think about it too. Perhaps . . . there may be something here that interests me after all. Good day, gentlemen.'

'Show them out,' Forrest snapped at me. But they were already halfway down the corridor, so I shuffled past them & got to the front door & opened it.

The rattle of carriages sent a wave of dust into my face.

Greye lumbered down the steps but his lordship

stopped by me. He said quietly, 'Forrest must be a difficult man to work for.'

My desire to punch him came right back.

He gave his cool smirk, took something out of his pocket & handed it to me. 'Meet me tonight at ten. I have an offer to make you. I think it will interest an ambitious man.'

I took the card. That was my big mistake. I turned away. Then back. 'What offer?'

He just smiled. We stood face to face, & we were the same age, & the same height, & if my father had not gambled everything away we would both have been wealthy young men. But he was richer than Satan & I was a madman's apprentice. He sauntered off down the street.

I shut the door & stood in the dark hall & read the card. It said

GIBSON'S ASSEMBLY ROOMS
Pursuits & Refreshments for Gentlemen of Taste.
Hot Bath Street, Aquae Sulis.

I scraped my cheek with it thoughtfully. The very place Sylvia had fled from. Probably a gambling den. Hardly the place for Compton to offer me a job. Still, anything would be better than this madhouse.

In the workroom I could hear Forrest raging against his fate. 'Ignorant arrogant fools . . . surely we can do without their stinking money . . .' Fragments of his wrath came scorching out, but he had brought it all on himself, with his druid folly & his naive kindness. I leaned against the door & listened. Ralph Alleyn's soothing tones oozed through the opening.

'They will reconsider. Be calm, John. It will work out.'

I heard Forrest give a wheezy laugh. He was silent a while. Then he said, 'I don't know what I'd do without you, old friend.'

'We will succeed. We have built our hospital, and soon we will make this a city where even the poor have fine homes. It's not a dream, John. You are making this happen.'

It was low & heartfelt. I turned away, uneasy.

Then I looked up. At the top of the stairs the girl was sitting on the highest step, watching me. 'Don't eavesdrop, Master Peacock,' she said. 'You might hear the truth about yourself.'

I shrugged. 'So might you.'

She laughed, a saucy laugh. 'I know it all. I just won't be telling it to you.'

As she stood I said, 'You know the rich boy too. What are you really here for, Sylvia?'

She was still a minute. Then she walked into the drawing room & slammed the door.

Well. She might have taken Forrest in, but not me. She's no little innocent.

This might be getting interesting.

Bladud

I can't tell you how long I lived by the water.
Its warmth was a wonder, as if the sun had sunk secretly into
the ground. Although it was winter I lived in a small hollow
of steamy heat, where summer plants bloomed in the soaked
earth. Snow melted as soon as it fell.
I drank, I washed, I scrubbed at my raw skin.
The water became all I had lost. The warmth of humans.
The soothing of speech.
I felt it ripple in my hands, slither through my arms. Like
something living. Like a girl.
And sometimes, in delirium or half asleep, I thought I saw
her, the spirit of the spring, standing over me and watching
me, clothed with green algae, her hair weed, her face sharp
and laughing and full of secrets.
Slowly, over weeks, I unfolded.
I walked upright.
I ate the plants and beasts that haunted the place.
On a day of blue sky, I cleared the algae and lichens of the

sacred spring, and I knelt down and bent over it and among
the bubbles I saw my face.

For a long time I stared.

Tears ran warm down my clear skin and fell into the spring.
There were no more scabs, no pustules, no oozing sores. I was
cured, and I felt my strength gather even in the bones and
nerves of my body.

And she was standing behind me, her shadow darkening the
water.

I said, 'What payment must I make to Sulis?'

Her answer bubbled from the depths of the world.

'Encircle my wildness. Hold me in a circle of stone.'

Sulis

She looked at herself in the mirror. The uniform was simple – black trousers, black sweatshirt with *Roman Baths Museum* on it, and the famous image of the gorgon head that had been found here and that they used as their logo.

The clothes were featureless and she was glad. She wished there had been a cap, or something to pull down over her eyes, but that was silly.

As she stood in the cold staff cloakroom she wondered if all jobs were so easy to get. Was this how the world worked – you knew someone who knew someone? The interview had taken less than ten minutes. The woman, Ruth, had looked stressed and in a hurry; she'd checked a few facts, name, age, the fake ID, and then said, 'Right, well the sooner you can start the better. Tomorrow?'

Sulis had said, 'I'd rather Monday.'

'Fantastic. Seven thirty sharp please. I'll get someone to take you round.'

She had needed the weekend to reassure herself about the man. When she'd left the building on Friday the pavement table had been empty. She'd slipped into the crowd of tourists, and to be completely safe she'd taken a long, looping walk home, doubling back in the streets and ducking down alleyways and cobbled lanes.

Then she'd gone up to her room and out on to the secret ledge on the roof; crouched down and holding tight to the giant stone acorn she'd kept a watch on the Circus for at least half an hour, intent on every stroller and vehicle, until Hannah had pulled up in the car below, and come up the stairs and called, 'Su? Are you in?' and she'd found herself stiff and cold, one arm gone to sleep, her mind a strange blank.

No loitering man. Nothing unusual.

Nothing on Saturday.

Nothing on Sunday.

But she must have been too quiet, because Simon insisted they all go out on Sunday afternoon for what he called a family outing. It turned out to be a visit to a country house he was interested in, but she had enjoyed the vast green lawns and the woods with their falling leaves, and the cream tea in the cosy tearoom afterwards.

Now, opening the door into the echoing hall of the museum, she told herself she'd imagined the man's interest in her. She had to get the old fear out of her mind, but it was hard. It lurked inside her, like a coldness in her chest, and though she could chat and laugh and seem normal, every time she was alone or the conversation flagged or a programme on the TV stopped for the ads, there it was.

Like a shadow.

'Are you Sulis?'

It was the boy with the security badge. 'I'm Josh. They've told me to give you the quick tour.'

He seemed a bit embarrassed by it all. 'Fine,' she said, as coolly as she could. 'Lead on.'

He wasn't a great guide. He went too fast and didn't explain things properly, as if he had other, more important things on his mind.

He led her down a corridor and outside on to a terrace of stone. 'There it is,' he muttered.

She stared in amazement. Below her a vast rectangular pool of hot water steamed in the crisp autumn air. It seemed deep but it was hard to tell, because the water was the palest emerald green. Tiny trails of bubbles rose here and there to its surface.

She stared round at its paved edges, the classical columns, the statues. 'Is all this Roman?'

'First daft question.' Josh leaned on the rail. 'The bath is. The rest is later. This was the Romans' outdoor swimming pool.'

'Where does the water come from? How does it get so hot?' Suddenly she realized how little she really knew about any of this, despite the quick research in Sheffield.

'Deep underground. It gets hot down there. I don't know how. The earth's core is warm, isn't it?' Suddenly he straightened, posed like a lecturer and adopted a voice of ridiculous poshness. 'The King's Bath spring is a natural water source which rises from deep under the city. It flows at a rate of a third of a million gallons a day and has never been known to fail.'

She giggled. He said, 'Quiet at the back please! The temperature of the water is a constant 49 degrees C. The water you are looking at is ancient. It fell as rain on the Mendip hills 6000 years ago and . . .'

'Is that true?'

'Well, it's what the guides tell the groups.' His voice trailed back to normal. He turned and walked on.

'Are you a guide?'

'No. But I want to be because the pay's better. And you get tips.'

'I don't think I could remember all that stuff.'

He shrugged but she could see he was pleased. 'If you had to say it ten times a day you would. Down here.'

They were underground now. She trailed behind him through dark rooms full of exhibits, cases of Roman pottery and gravestones, altars, models and reconstructions, the broken life of the ancient bathers. Josh came back. 'Bored, or bored?'

'I like it actually.'

'We're right under the square now. All those tourists and buskers and shops are about ten metres above us.

Wait here a minute, will you?'

While she waited the thought of the pavement tables, the man's dark eyes on hers through the crowd. For a moment she almost felt she was being watched again; she glanced round, but the museum was dim and shadowy, and there was no one here but her.

Something clicked, among the cases.

'Josh?'

There *was* someone watching her. She felt his eyes, the intent, secret scrutiny. Her hands were resting on one of the information panels; she was gripping it so tight her fingers hurt.

'Who's there?' she whispered.

Half-lit glass. Reflections of cups and Roman gemstones. A flat stone pavement, stretching into the dark.

Then she looked up, and saw the eyes.

They were stone, and they stared at her from a face, the strangely circular face of a frowning man with flowing moustaches and a corona of flames bursting out all around him. Or were they snakes? In the dimness it was hard to tell. But suddenly, as if Josh was switching everything on, spotlights erupted in a fused focus, and she saw that the face stared from the fragments of a broken pediment. And behind it, faintly, were two great wings.

For a moment something moved in her, deep in the shadows of her memory. She hugged herself. She wanted to cry out. Instead she whispered, her voice tiny in the underground chamber.

I know it's you. You told Caitlin she could fly. Why did you do that? She was my friend. You killed her.

Light.

A burst of music.

A voice rang out. 'Welcome to the Roman Baths Museum. Our interactive displays are now open and we invite you to . . .'

'Sulis?'

Josh had come round a corner and was staring at her curiously.

Normality clicked back with a jolt that seemed to jar right through her nerves; she breathed out smoothly and said, 'I just dropped my watch. I don't think it's broken.' She pretended to fasten it, her fingers controlled now, the shaking gone.

For a moment he watched, as if he wasn't quite convinced. He said, 'This place can give you the creeps in the dark.'

She turned. 'Can it?'

Maybe her voice was cooler than she'd meant, because he looked almost hurt. Then he said, 'Come on. We'll be opening in ten minutes.'

He showed her the rest of the rooms, but nothing really interested her until they came to the place where the water poured out from a great arched overflow, a roaring, steamy place that she could look at through a grille. She gripped the warm metal and pressed her forehead against it. 'Look at all the coins!'

'People throw them in. Offerings.' He grinned. 'At the end of the season we clean them out and split the profit between the staff. Mind, you get all sorts of junk. Foreign coins. Buttons. You'd think they'd show a goddess more respect.'

The heat was wonderful. A moist glow on her face and lips, like how she imagined a sauna must be. But they had to leave it, and as he led her back to the main hall he said, 'Ruth said you were a student.'

Immediately she was on her guard. 'I'm starting uni in October.'

'Here?'

'Yes.'

'Most people move away.'

'We've only just moved here.'

He said, 'From the North. I can tell by your accent.'

She made herself smile. 'Is it that obvious?'

'Well, compared to the locals.'

He was silent after that. As she followed him down the corridor she felt she had to be friendly back, so she said, 'Are you a student?'

He didn't answer, and she couldn't see his face. Then he said, 'No. Looking for a job.'

There was a warning note she recognized. It meant, don't ask me about this, and she knew exactly how that felt. When they reached the entrance hall he said,

'Good luck,' and wandered off to open the doors to the public, and she went into the gift shop to start work.

It wasn't too difficult. By lunchtime she had got the hang of where everything was, the stationery, the tea towels, the expensive copies of Roman statues and jewellery. She couldn't operate the till yet, but Ruth said they'd teach her that soon enough, and could she just concentrate today on learning the stock, please, and the prices, and keeping it tidy, and watching the schoolkids who came through in great excited waves breaking over the sharpeners and pencils and tiny Roman soldiers.

At lunchtime she needed some fresh air, so she took her sandwiches out to Queen's Square where there was a green space and some benches to sit on, and lots of people admiring the superb buildings. Simon had told her that this was Jonathan Forrest's first great masterpiece. 'He did it before the Circus. Fabulous work.'

She sat in her coat and watched the leaves drift from the trees. Already she felt reasonably happy with the job; she liked seeing the tourists from all over the world puzzling over prices and trying to make themselves understood with phrases from guidebooks; she loved the mystery of the hot springs. For a moment she had a flicker of something that had worried her earlier . . . yes, that stone face. She glanced down at the logo on her sweatshirt. But she couldn't remember now why it had alarmed her and she dismissed it and wondered if there would be time to go to Boots and get some moisturizer before she had to get back.

And then she saw him.

Every bone in her body seemed to petrify.

He was standing on the other side of the square, and he had his back to her, but she recognized the dark coat, so long it came below his knees. He was looking down at another one of the pigs dotted round the city, this one of transparent Perspex, so you almost didn't know it was there.

She stood, grabbing the bag that fell from her lap, shoving the half-eaten sandwich inside. The Coke tin hit the ground and spilled.

He had not moved. But then she saw him reach out and touch the invisible pig, touch it lightly and run his finger over its surface. For a moment she almost felt the cold, slightly damp plastic. He raised his hand, held it up, its back to her, as if in greeting.

He must be able to see her. Reflected.

She turned and ran, pushing people out of the way, barging out of the gate and across the road, so heedless that a driver blared his horn at her angrily, and another braked hard. Ignoring the lights at the crossing she sprinted along the pavement, round a corner and into a short cut she'd found, through the linked courtyards of an ancient almshouse, back out into a street lined with charity shops. She dived into the nearest, grabbed a skirt, gasped, 'Can I try this on please?' and slid into the changing room, yanking the curtain across so hard it almost fell off.

Her heart was thudding. Breathless, she waited, her back against the mirror. After an anguished minute she opened the curtain a slit, and peered out. There were a few people in the shop. The doorway was empty.

She didn't know what to do. Unless she phoned Hannah! As soon as the thought came she threw the musty skirt on the chair and dug out the mobile but stopped with it in her hand.

No. Stupid. She was panicking.

She imagined Hannah screeching up in the car and running inside, all scared, and the people in the shop . . . No. Take a breath.

Get a grip.

She sneaked another look out. The doorway was still empty. She sat on the wobbly stool and waited. There were ten minutes before she needed to be back at the museum, and she could make it in two from here.

There was a song on the radio. An old Bowie song. She let the music flow into her, concentrating on it, letting it take her somewhere else. Music always helped.

The curtain rattled. She jumped up.

'Have you finished in there, dear? Only there's someone else . . .'

'Yes. Sorry.' She opened the curtain cautiously. The elderly woman from the counter stood there with another pensioner. They both looked at her, as if there was something strange about her. She made herself smile brightly. 'Doesn't fit. Sorry.'

The skirt was hideous, she realized. As she put it back on the rack she almost laughed, and felt a cold shivery hysteria.

She stepped into the street and straight into him.

He said, 'Not a very cool shop.'

Sulis took a breath. 'Josh.' She glanced up the street.

He had a sausage roll in some greasy paper. He took a bite. 'I'm not following you, if that's what you think.'

'I . . .'

'Joke.'

'Right.'

He looked at her closely. 'You all right?'

'Fine. Better get back.'

She walked, fast. He fell into step beside her. She managed a few paces, then couldn't help looking back. She looked back again twice before they came to the square, and then as they walked through the crowd her eyes darted quickly at the faces of the people.

'Someone chasing you?' Josh said.

She gave him one glare. Then she pushed open the swing door and ran inside.

Of course, she thought later, putting a book into a bag for a customer, she wasn't safe even in the museum. There was nothing to stop him coming in, buying something, bringing it to the till, standing over her, looking down. He had been tall. So tall. But then she'd only been a kid.

He didn't come. All afternoon she was on edge, and when the time came for the shop to close she couldn't wait for the bolts to be shot home on the street door.

Ruth pulled the blind down and turned in relief. 'God. What a hectic afternoon. Now the schools are back it's worse. I think I'll emigrate.'

She came over and said, 'Well, Sulis, How was your first day?'

'Fine thanks.' She managed a smile.

'Well you did a lot better than most. See you tomorrow.'

She went to the staffroom and took her coat, wary of meeting Josh, but there were only a few of the guides chatting, so she slid carefully out of the staff entrance and looked round.

The street was empty. She took a deep breath, and ran.

It took her ten minutes to run far enough through the tangled streets and upper terraces of the city to be sure she was safe. Finally, her side aching, she stopped for breath, holding on to a black wrought-iron railing.

She wanted suddenly to crouch down on the floor and hug herself tight, because that was what she had always done when she was small, after thinking about the man, and Caitlin.

Sometimes she had dragged a blanket from the bed

and curled under it for hours, counting and singing and drawing spirals and circles on paper, not coming out despite all the promises the foster-mothers had held out. Counsellors had talked to her about it. 'Do you feel safe there, sweetheart? Can I just peep in and talk to you for a minute?'

She straightened from the railings.

He wouldn't destroy her. She wouldn't let that happen.

But could it really be him?

She walked the rest of the way slowly and firmly, not looking round.

Turning into the Circus her heart lifted, just a little, at the perfection of the circle of houses. But the walk round would be curved, and suddenly she didn't want that, she wanted a straight line, so she strode directly across the lumpy circle of lawn in the centre, under the five great trees.

Leaves clogged the grass. She kicked her feet through drifts of golden and copper crispness. Under the trees the grass was sparser. In the very centre the concrete roof of some underground structure was lichen-green.

'Sulis!' Simon stood on the house steps with his key and a bag full of groceries. He waved, and as she came over he said, 'Had a good day in the working world?'

'It was great.'

He glanced at her, then opened the door. As she slipped in after him she felt something crunch under her

72

feet on the floor like shavings of wood. But it was only a few leaves, blown inside. As she watched, a draught gusted one lightly to the foot of the stairs.

Oak leaves.

Though there were no oaks in the Circus.

Zac

As I was eating Cook's dire gruel in the kitchen next morning, Forrest came in & said, 'Get yourself a warm coat on, Zac. We're going out.'

I looked up. 'To the site?' I had no interest in the place, because all it was yet was a tilted muddy field above the town. Workmen were toiling to make it flat, digging out an enormous ledge for the circular street to rest on. If, indeed, it was ever completed.

'Not the site.' My master held out his hands to the fire in the hearth. His hands are often cold, I notice. Also his asthma is worst in the mornings. 'We're going to Stanton Drew.'

'Is that some village?'

He laughed. As did Cook, & even the skivvy smirked. Which is what I despise about Forrest's house. A gentleman should not eat in the kitchen, but we all do, because his dining table is a mess of plans & books.

'A village, yes, but that's not why we go. I have business

there, & need the help of my assistant surveyor. It will be good training for you.'

I assumed there was some fine house to be inspected & so nodded, abandoning the spoon in the cold gruel. But as I went out he said, 'You'll need a bag. We will not return till tomorrow.'

Running up to my small room I wondered what had put him in so good a temper. After the farrago with Compton I would have thought he would be savage with frustration, but he was as changeable as the wind.

I threw my nightshirt & fresh linen & some money in my leather bag. It's a worn, expensive thing & I love the feel & smell of it, because it was bought for my father when he was a young man setting off for Europe, to tour the wonders of Paris and Rome. Which was something I too had sworn I would do when I had made back all the money he had gambled away.

The thought of my lost inheritance brought on that tightness in the mind that I know is anger – a hard unspoken anger against my father's stupid, stupid act. So to drive it away I sat & pulled on my boots & thought of Forrest. What was the meaning of the word Oroboros? Why the serpent eating its tail? I planned to wait until Forrest was out & then consult his books on druidry & his heaps of musty antiquarian pamphlets. If there was some secret meaning I meant to know it.

The landing creaked.

I paused, one boot half on. Then I stood & hopped

to the door & flung it open.

The landing was empty. But there was a trace of rose scent in the air.

'Stop spying on me,' I roared. There was no sign of her, but I knew she could hear me.

'If you touch any of my possessions I'll tell Forrest and have you thrown back on the streets!'

A faint giggle, up the attic stair.

I went back in & slammed the door. What was he thinking of taking in such a creature! All over the city the rumour had run. Did he want to destroy his business? Not that I cared either way. What was his business to me? But then I remembered a dream I had had in the night, just a fragment of it, of the great circle of houses standing in the sun, filled with people, its centre green with five tall trees. And grudgingly I knew I would like to see the Circus built.

We set off at ten, riding the only two horses he kept. At the corner I looked back & saw Sylvia waving from the doorstep. She wore a blue shawl against the cold & there was a pert smile on her lips. Forrest waved back. I looked away.

In the stink & filth of the old part of the city I was glad to be a little above the throng, but in the fashionable streets we made better progress. I was able to see the more eminent citizens parading, ladies in the latest modes & men with fast curricles & carriages. A dashing barouche drawn by a pair of glossy black mares came by us at speed, rattling over the stone bridge. I glimpsed a handsome man at the reins; he glanced at us as he passed.

'Lord Compton in a hurry,' I said, remembering the card he had given me. I had still not decided whether to go.

Forrest snorted. I had hoped he would make some comment, but he said nothing. He takes his disappointments bitterly to heart.

I prompted him. 'Will he invest, do you think?'

'If he does not I'll build the Circus anyway.'

I stared at him. 'With your own money?'

'Why not? I can certainly sell the building contracts. I tell you, Zac, my street of the sun will be the finest street you have ever seen. I will lay out the secrets of the ancients like sigils on the land. I have wanted all my life to create such a city. A puppy like Compton won't stand in my way.'

I was silent. It would be risky to proceed without investors. If he was to lose everything I would be out of my apprenticeship & back to poverty. Perhaps he saw my doubt, because he gave me his rare smile. 'But we are out of town, Zac. Now we can ride!'

It was a glorious day. Cold for autumn, so that the wind stung tears to my eyes, but the sky was blue & the leaves gusted around us in great golden tempests. We climbed by steep paths up to the downs, scattering the great flocks of sheep that grazed amiably, & disturbing

hares that fled as we rode by. From here we could see all
the city below, the way it huddled in the saucer of its
hills, the tangle of roofs & chimneys around the hidden
hot spring at its heart.

'Do you know the story of Bladud?' Forrest
asked suddenly.

'I never heard it,' I said wearily, knowing I was
about to.

'He was a king & a druid and he suffered from a
terrible illness. Leprosy, perhaps. His people cast him out,
& he wandered these hills in great distress, in the cold
& rain, & the only work he could get was as a swineherd.
But he saw that the pigs he guarded went each day to a
spring in a valley & rolled in the water, which came
from the earth hot, & that it kept their skins pure &
white. So he enticed them out with acorns & entered the
water himself.'

'And was cured.' The ending was obvious. I wondered
that he believed such old flim-flam.

He looked at me as if my curtness had spoiled it for
him. Then he said, 'Yes. He was cured.' He turned the
horse & walked on & I came after him. I felt a little sorry,
so I said, 'And that is how the spring came to be a site of
cures, I suppose. But this was when the Romans were in
these lands?'

'Before. Long before.' He sounded terse but I knew he
could not help himself on this subject, & soon his
enthusiasm burst out. 'I believe this was a place of magic

78

long before the Romans. That the druids ruled a great kingdom here. We have theories of this – if we could dig below the baths who knows what might be found. And we believe . . .'

'We?' I said.

He fell silent. We had come to a gate & he leaned down to open it, his gloved hand slipping on the frosty wood. 'Other antiquaries. Fellow scholars.'

He considered himself a scholar. It was true he had written books. And yet he had never been to the university, as my father had, or as I had been intended to, So, out of spite, I said, 'Like Master Stukeley?'

'Stukeley!' His anger was explosive. 'That fool wouldn't know scholarship if it fell on him like a tree! And his drawing of Stone-henge! A child could do better. Don't mention that toad's name to me, Zac, I cannot bear the man.'

He rode in front of me & I confess I smirked at his back. My master's book on the druids had been mocked by this Stukeley, who had called its ideas 'Whimseys of a crack'd imagination'. And yet they were both as crack'd as each other to me.

It took just over an hour to reach the turnpike road. We clopped along it between overgrown hedges until we turned aside at a tiny conical tollhouse where the payment was a farthing each. The lane led down into a village tucked into a crook of the downs, its church tower rising above trees & its small sluggish river crossed by a wooden bridge. As we clattered over I looked for the great house, but I could see none. It seemed a poor, mangey sort of place.

We turned between two hovels of cottages. A snot-nosed boy ran out & stared at us as if he'd never seen such things as men before.

'This is it,' Forrest said. And dismounted.

I confess I thought he was jesting. My expression must have told of my disgust because he looked up & said softly, 'You must climb down from your high horse, Zac, if you want to work with me. I am not a man for airs & graces.'

I wanted to say something scornful & angry. But I bit my tongue & swung down, my boots splatting in the unspeakable filth.

Forrest bent to the boy. 'Remember me, sirrah?'

The child nodded & grinned. He had few teeth.

'Then we will have the same arrangement as before. Lead our horses to the inn & have them stabled & come to me for the pennies. We'll be at the stones.'

He hauled his bag of surveying instruments down.

My heart plummeted. 'Stones?'

He cast me a sidelong look. 'Did you expect some mansion, sir? Well, I'll show you one.'

He led me over a stile in the hedge, & when I was across it & picking its splinters from my hand I found myself in a field lumpy with dried dung & fallen leaves. Sheep stood & stared at us. A few moved away & bleated, uneasily. The sound set a crowd of jackdaws racketing in the trees.

Forrest stopped. 'There, Zac.' His voice was awestruck. 'Is that not the masterpiece of some long-dead architect?'

The field was littered with stones. They were enormous, leaning, fallen. The nearest to me was made of some red conglomerate, a massy lichened thing higher than my head, wider than I could put my arms round. I stared at its pitted surface, pocked & pustuled with holes. I said, 'The ancients liked their materials rough.'

Forrest laughed. 'Indeed. The fashionable ladies of Aquae Sulis would never tolerate it. But these stones are no haphazard mess. They form circles.'

He walked among them, & I gazed around. The space was enormous, almost as great as the centre of our Circus would be. The stones stood like slewed cubes of grey in the gently sloping field. They were meaningless, would take winches & rope & oxen to move. And yet he was right. It was a circle.

'I have surveyed this place before – I think I was the first to do so properly,' Forrest said, dumping his bag in a patch of bare grass. 'No one else has cared for it, but it was important once, Zac. Look at its proportions! It cannot have been built to live in. That makes no sense. There is this circle . . . the Great Circle, let us call it. Then, over there, more stones. I found two smaller circles, which I have called the North-east & the South-west. Those are in better condition – one has a flat slab, like an altar. Great ceremonies must have taken place in them. Vast gatherings of wise men, maybe women too. Then there are stones outside them which may be roads for processions of druids to walk along.'

He was on it again, his hobby-horse. I was hungry, & longing for some food. 'Did druids have inns?' I asked, carelessly.

He turned to me & for a moment I knew I had goaded him to anger. Oddly, that pleased me. He snapped, 'We have work to do, sir. Let's get on with it.'

If he had already surveyed it why do it all over again? We spent the whole afternoon checking his measurements, unrolling long tapes & walking backwards with the sighting poles, so that my boots stank with sheep dung. It was biting cold too, the wind rising & whipping the long skirts of my coat against my legs, flapping my collar. Forrest seemed unconscious of the weather; he worked like a man absorbed, pacing & drawing, & sometimes just standing with one hand on one of the stones as if he could feel something that moved deep inside it.

By sunset the wind was almost a gale. Banks of dark cloud were building up on the horizon; as I packed the equipment I watched them anxiously. 'We should go. There will be a storm.'

'Soon, Zac.' He was scrabbling in the mud with a small trowel.

I wrapped my arms about me & began to pace to & fro, my feet frozen to numbness. Then I crossed to the smaller circle. It was certainly easier to see its shape & the avenue that led to it. Nine or ten vast stones remained, & I climbed up on the fallen one, feeling the gritty surface splotched with its powdery lichens. A tree grew next to it, a great oak tree, huge and strong. The gale was sending its leaves down in showers of copper & bronze. I picked up an acorn from the ground, & held it in my gloved hand, wondering at the extraordinary way each tree has its own shape, its own design.

'Musing on time, Zac?' Forrest was watching me, his steady eyes calm.

I tossed the acorn & put it in my pocket. 'Only on the time when we'll get something to eat.'

He nodded, a little sadly. 'Ah yes. I'm sorry. I get caught up in the excitement of such places. And it is so apt for this tree to be here, because the oak is the druids' holy tree, did you know that? But it's raining, & you're very wet. Come on. The inn's delights await us.'

I trudged after him. More extraordinary than the acorn is a man who can find stones in a muddy field a place of excitement. As I shouldered the bag of tools I let the ache of self-pity come over me – a thing I try to avoid usually, because it has no purpose. And yet there is a sort of pleasure in it. I thought of home, my mother's room, with the warm fire & my two sisters sitting beside it, probably reading or sewing or doing all the useless things girls do.

And in the study along the corridor my father would be standing by the window gazing out on the rainy park, perhaps with a glass of wine in his hand, sighing over his sold paintings & his auctioned racehorses. And his son who must learn a trade.

A son shouldn't despise his father. And perhaps I love him still. But like Forrest my disappointment is still bitter, & I do not have his crazy dreams of the perfect city to help me forget.

The inn was another tragedy. I had expected at least a posting house, with some bustle & coaches, but it was a slipshod pig-poke of a place, the thatch sliding from its eaves, & only a bare room inside with a few settles, stinking of ale & worse things. But the fire roared, & I went straight to it.

Forrest warmed his hands too, pulling off gloves and coat. Then he called, 'Mistress? Your guests are hungry.'

The woman who came out of the kitchen was as ample as I had ever seen. Greasy as she was from the spit, she flung her arms around him with a scream of joy that embarrassed him mightily.

'Master Forrest! So hale you look! And this – is this your son, sir? The picture of you.'

I don't which of us was more offended. Me, probably, because Forrest just laughed. 'No, Luce, this is not my son. Jack is abroad, studying architecture in Italy. This is Master Stoke, my assistant.'

I bowed.

She gave me a straight look. 'A fine gennleman to be sure.'

Forrest smiled. 'We'd like a room, Luce, & something hot. Just for tonight.' He took her aside, speaking quietly.

I turned, glowering into the fire. It was barely possible to understand the speech of these people, but I had seen enough. I was a stranger & would always be a stranger. Well, I could live with that.

I went up to the room to wash & found it an attic under the eaves, with three beds, but I prayed only Forrest & I would have to share it. Another snoring oaf would be too much. But who else would visit here? I poured out a little cold water & got the worst of the mud from my hands & face, then changed my shirt & coat. I wished I had other boots, but these would have to do. By the time I had finished I was at least respectable, not that anyone in this hole could tell. I went to the window & threw open the shutter.

A great storm was rising. The wind laid all the trees & hedgerows down before it. There was a small orchard outside, grazed by a flock of geese, & to my dismay I saw there were stones here too, three great ones, huddled together. For a moment I was curious as to how they related to the circles, what their purpose had been, but then weariness with the whole thing came over me & I went & lay on the frowsty bed. Rain pattered on the thatch. I wondered how much lower I could sink than this.

My apprenticeship with Forrest had been arranged by a friend of my father's – perhaps the one friend he had left. It was to be a new life for me – a new start for my family. I was to make the fortune we had lost. I had felt the faint stirrings of interest, on hearing of Forrest's alleged genius, but meeting him had been a sore disappointment, & now with this trollop he had brought to the house, & the rich men of the city despising his new scheme, I wished I had never come. Perhaps I should write home & ask them to think again. I had no idea what fees my father was paying Forrest but I was sure they could be better spent. I would never be much of an architect.

I curled up. Failure & loneliness galled me. For a moment I felt like some outcast, like the leper king in the forest among the pigs, lost & seeking only a magic place of healing. Then Forrest called up the stairs, 'Supper, Zac!'

The food was, I suppose, surprisingly good. A crackling joint & mashed swede & turnip & a steaming confection that I had no name for but which tasted of cream & which banished the cold right out of me to the fingertips.

I sat back with a glass of porter & was almost content.

'So, Zac,' Forrest watched me. 'Did you see the connection between these circles & my work?'

I shrugged. 'A druid circle, sir, but . . .'

'There were thirty stones.' He stood & paced, impatient. 'Twenty-seven remain, but there were thirty in the outer ring, as at Stone-henge. As if that number was a magic one. As if it meant some harmony, some geometric truth. Three times ten. Perhaps they had thirty gods, or thirty ancestors, or thirty days in a month. It would make thirteen months in a year . . .'

I tried not to sigh. 'So you will have thirty houses in the Circus.'

'And three avenues leading out. The points of these will form a triangle of equal sides within the circle. The houses will have three storeys each. The pediment will be crowned with a circle of acorns – the fruit of the oak. Bladud's crown. This is what my desgn is, Zac, a repeat of what the ancients did. *I will build my own stone circle.*'

I drank. 'What Greye said. About the noise. The foul air . . .'

'Total nonsense.' He glared at me. 'Can you believe such rubbish?'

This from him, with his leper druids! The pot-woman had told us some tale that the stones here were the remains of wedding guests turned to stones for dancing on Sundays. He had laughed at that.

I said, 'People fear new things. Perhaps a straight terrace would be better. You would make a good profit, & then . . .'

He was looking at me as if I had stabbed him with a knife. He put the cup down. 'Get to bed. I have to go out for an hour. Don't wait up for me. Tomorrow we ride back early.'

He went out, slamming the door, & I stared at it in astonishment. Where was there to go in this pig-poke of a place? And yet at once it came to me that this was the real reason we had come, & the sign of the serpent devouring its tail flashed into my mind. In minutes I was up, had caught my coat & slipped out after him.

The storm was roaring over the downs. The orchard was a howling clamour of threshing branches. But I could see him. He had not gone far – he stood in the shelter of the three stones, & he had his horse with him, saddled & bridled as if he had ordered it earlier.

I cursed.

My own beast was tucked up for the night.

Just as I thought I should run to the stable, Forrest swung himself into the saddle, & I saw in the darkness flickers of light approach. I pressed myself back.

Men rode out of the night. I counted ten, fourteen. More. They went as silent as they could, just a clinking of harness & a shuffle of hooves, & the storm covered them, whipping their coats. Each was wellwrapped, a dark shape. They came to Forrest & words were spoken, a question was asked but I couldn't hear what, so I crept closer, behind the nearest great stone.

'*Oroboros.*' The answer was clear, shouted against the rising storm. Then the men were turning, & Forrest with them. I slid along the stone, my face to its coldness.

Hissing.

An eruption of spitting, an angry cackle at my feet!

I leapt back, cursing, my heart leaping wildly as the geese came at me, wings wide, necks outstretched, three white furious spectres in the night.

Forrest turned. He saw me. Our eyes met for a moment, through the rain, & I heard the man near him cry, 'Someone is there. Watching us!'

They would find me & drag me out. Someone drew out a sword, its blade glittering briefly in the lanternlight.

Forrest said, 'It's nothing but geese. We alarmed them.' He turned away from me.

I heard the rider say, 'Are you sure?'

'Sure. Let's go.'

I edged back from the hissing birds into the stone's darkness as the men streamed by me, a cavalcade of shadows. After the last was gone & only the storm was left, I backed to the inn door & found it open.

The fat woman was leaning there, one arm on the lintel.

'A zore night for a fine laddie to be out in things that don't conzern 'e,' she drawled.

I pushed past her.

She smelt. She laughed at my back.

Bladud

So I began to build.

The first step was to clear the ground. I dug and toiled in the heat of summer.

I moved stones. I uprooted brambles and rushes and reeds. Waterfowl squawked out of my way.

I was careful. The ground was holy and its inhabitants were hers.

And yet as the opening was widened the waters came rising up, welling warm, and the heat of them was sometimes too hard to bear so that my fingers were scorched and I gasped for breath.

If magic is a word for the unknown, then this was magic.

I had unlocked the heat of the earth's heart, the lands deep below us, the places men dream of in the night, when they toss and turn and wake in fear.

This was a heat with nothing human in it.

One day, when I turned round, a boy was watching me from the greenwood. For hours he watched me, and then, when I

was so tired I sat down to rest, he came and took the antler
pick and began to work in my place.

'Master,' he said, 'a druid should not dig.'

I sat and smiled in my weariness.

Next day, my people came. They came with picks and levers
and ropes of twisted hemp. They came with songs for the
spirit, with flowers and fruit and skulls for her.

The spring welled into a pool.

Its rim was stone, cut and curved. Thirty stones, to hold her
wildness in place.

The people stood back, and waited.

All around I planted acorns. For her crown.

The Foundations

*Architecture is a term under which is comprehended all the
Causes and Rules of Building.*

Sulis

'All right?'

She turned, quickly. 'Fine, thanks.'

'Only I thought you looked a bit . . .'

'What?'

Josh shrugged. Then he said, 'Scared.'

She had her coat and scarf on and a woolly hat that came down close over her eyes. Outside it was raining, the square windswept, the tables stacked by the cafe in rickety heaps. The tourists had gone home.

The word annoyed her. 'Don't be ridiculous.'

'Right. See you.' He walked away down the marble hall, but she took a step after him at once.

'Josh, I'm sorry. I didn't mean to say that.'

He turned. Then he came back. He was taller than her and very thin, all wristbones and cheekbones, as if he didn't eat enough. She realized she knew very little about him, and yet in the week that she'd worked in the museum he'd been the only one who'd really talked to her.

And yes. She was scared.

He said, 'Tell you what. I'll get my stuff and we'll go and get some coffee. Then I'll walk you home.'

That was the last thing she wanted. But she had already said, 'OK.'

While he was gone she stood by the window and looked out. It was a wild evening, already autumnal. All around her the buildings were masses of shadow, their Georgian doorways and casements lit by dripping glimmers of light from the lampposts. A few late workers hurried by under umbrellas. She watched them carefully.

The job was proving harder than she'd thought. Constantly having to talk to strangers, give them change, chat to them, had been fun at first, but after only a few days the fear of being watched had come back and stayed. If a woman glanced at her a little too closely or a man caught her eye and smiled, it turned her cold. Because he was out there. Somewhere.

Josh came back. 'OK?'

'Fine.'

They went out by the front door. Tom, the night guard, muttered, 'Aye aye! He doesn't waste much time, does he?' to Sulis as he unlocked. She laughed, but Josh said nothing, and outside he walked quickly across the square as if annoyed.

She hurried after him. 'He didn't mean anything.'

'He's a pain. You don't have to work with him.' He paused in the rain. 'Which way?'

'Up the hill.'

'Good. I've got to go to the bookshop.'

'You read?'

He managed a smile. 'No, I just look at the pictures.'

They walked up past the closing shops, the flapping canvas of the market stalls. Rain pattered on the plastic covers of postcards; Sulis caught the frown of the gorgon face through the trickling drops.

Josh was silent. Really they were strangers, she thought. She had no idea what to say. And he walked fast. Always a little ahead of her.

He said, 'Must be strange, moving so far.'

'What do you mean?'

'Well, Sheffield's a big city . . .'

She almost stopped walking. 'How did you know . . . ?'

'Ruth said.'

'She shouldn't have said.' Sulis caught up with him. 'Have you been talking about me?' Her breath was tight.

Josh laughed. 'Everyone gets talked about in that place. Don't worry about it.'

Rain dripped down her fingers. She shoved her hands in her pockets. 'It's just . . .'

'Really. No one's said anything bad.' He looked uneasy now.

After a minute she said, 'Don't tell anyone, will you?'

'What?'

'Where I came from. Don't.'

Josh shrugged. At the bookshop he said, 'I won't be long.'

'Take your time.' She was glad to stand in the blast of heat at the entrance.

'It's upstairs.' He strode off quickly between the tables of bestsellers. She stared after him, the word *Sheffield* ringing like the echo of an alarm in her head. But it was nothing. It meant nothing.

There were a few people browsing – she studied each of them carefully. None of them were him.

She moved towards the stairs along the shelf labelled Crime, trailing her hand over copies of Agatha Christie. She'd seen some of these on television. Bodies in the library, murder on the Orient Express. Scornful, she flipped one with her finger. What did they know? How many of these writers had witnessed a murder, seen a girl fall out into the blue emptiness of the sky, arms wide, screaming?

She stopped beside a tall mirror, seeing her own face.

And there behind her, on a shelf. *The photograph*.

For a moment she couldn't move. The shock was too great. The startled gaze of the little girl caught in the flash met her like a challenge.

Then she turned and snatched the book up.

It was called *Bizarre Mysteries and Strange Deaths*.

She glanced around. No one was near; the stairs were empty.

The book was thick, a paperback. The photograph was in black and white, so that the little girl looked unnaturally pale, her hand in the policewoman's grip white as a ghost's.

Sulis touched it. Her fingers – those same fingers – lingered on the face, closed tight on the spine. She wanted to steal the book, cram it into her bag, so that no one else would see it. Her back was cold with sweat because the book felt like a grenade, a trembling explosive that might detonate and destroy her life. Carefully, she turned it over.

A fascinating account of recent real-life unsolved cases including . . .

Her eyes flew down the list until she came to

. . . The Flying Girl, the mysterious case of Caitlin Morgan and M . . .

'I didn't know you were into that tack,' Josh said, running down the stairs.

She dropped the book. It crashed to the floor and he bent and picked it up.

Her heart thudded like a drum.

Josh turned the book over. He looked at the photograph.

She felt as if all the sound in the shop had faded, all the people had dwindled to shadows, all the universe focused down to his gaze on the hated image.

He would recognize her.

The Perfect City would fracture like a cracked mirror.

He said, 'Grisly stuff. Murders!'

'I knocked it off the shelf. By accident. I was just picking it up.' She licked dry lips, knowing she was talking too much. 'I didn't want to read it or anything. Yuk! Are you kidding!'

'Mmm.' His eyes were fixed on the little girl's face.

Desperate, she said, 'Did you get what you wanted?'

There was a plastic bag under his arm. 'Yes thanks.' Slowly he propped *Bizzare Mysteries* back on the shelf and said, 'There's a coffee place upstairs. We can sit in the window and look down at the street. If you like.'

'Fine.'

Anything. Anywhere but here. She ran up the stairs and into the cafe, pulling out her purse, her heart still thudding in her chest, her ears ringing as if a silent bomb had exploded right beside her. Had he recognized her? He could never have done. Could he?

They both had hot chocolate, and Josh insisted on extra sugar in his, which she said was disgusting, and then they sat at a round, ring-stained table and looked down at the slanted umbrellas and cars. Sulis sipped the hot drink; it scalded her tongue.

Josh's phone burbled. He took it out, read the message and switched it off. Then he said, 'Better?'

'What?'

'Well, it's quiet up here. No one but us.'

She glanced at the girl reading a magazine behind the counter. 'So?'

'So tell me.'

Cold, she stared.

He shrugged, impatient. 'Come on, Sulis, what do you think you're hiding? You were white as a sheet down there and you ran up here like scared cat. And at work you're always . . .'

'What?' She was angry now.

He rubbed the tabletop with a grubby finger. 'Watchful. I've seen you. Always checking people out. As if there's someone you don't want to meet.'

'Right,' she said, acid. 'And who's that then? My ex-boyfriend? The school bully?'

'I think it's that weirdo.'

She looked up. 'Weirdo?' It came out as a whisper.

Josh shrugged and turned his cup in the saucer. He didn't look at her. 'I saw you dive into that shop the other day. I suppose I thought it was me you wanted to avoid, and so I hung about outside looking in the window, waiting for you. Just to embarrass you. But there was someone else waiting too. A thin bloke in a dark coat. He saw me looking at him and he walked off. But I recognized him, and I've seen him since. He hangs around outside the museum sometimes, watches the buskers, reads the paper, sits at the pavement tables. Once he came in on one of the tours.'

She was shaking. Her hands were icy on the hot cup. She put it down with a clatter.

'He was there again today.' Josh's voice was quiet.

Now he was looking at her. 'Outside, as we were closing, I saw him standing in the doorway of the Abbey. That's why I said I'd walk you home.' He was silent a moment. Then he said, 'It's none of my business. But if this guy is bothering you . . .'

'He's not.' She said it so sharply the girl at the counter looked up from reading.

Josh pulled a face. He sipped his sweet hot chocolate and said nothing.

Sulis felt sick. She was suddenly trapped, like a bird in a cage, as if there were bars every way she turned. A woman came in and ordered coffee; the espresso machine started up in a hiss and rattle of steam.

'All right.' She sat up and faced him. 'Maybe he is. But that's not all of it. You recognized me, didn't you? On the cover of that book.'

He stirred the chocolate. For a moment she knew she had made a terrible mistake. Then he said quietly, 'You haven't changed that much.'

Had he recognized her? Or was he covering his astonishment? She said, 'Listen to me, Josh. I can't talk here. I can't tell you here. But I need you to do something for me. Go downstairs and buy that book.'

He stared. 'I can't afford it.'

'I mean for me.' She was groping in her bag; had the money out. She pushed it across the table. 'I don't want it there. I don't want people looking at it . . .'

Josh put his spoon down. Whatever he saw in her

face seemed to alarm him. 'You don't want this guy to see it?'

'Anyone.'

'Is he some sort of reporter? Police?'

'I'll tell you! I promise. I'll explain everything. Just go, Josh, please! Now! Just get it off the shelf!'

The rising panic in her voice was clear, even to her. She pushed the note closer and he took it. He stood up.

'You will tell me?'

'Yes. Yes!'

'All right. Wait here. Don't go anywhere.'

'I won't. Just be quick.'

When he was gone she pushed the chocolate away with a shiver. What if the book was gone? If someone had bought it? It must have been there for days, maybe weeks. And in other shops, all over the country, were hundreds of identical copies – her face staring out from shelf after shelf.

She realized she was rocking gently in the chair. Because she had done it now – she'd promised to tell him. And if she did someone else would know about Caitlin and her and him. Unless she went, at once. Forget the job. Just completely vanish.

She stood, grabbing her coat, but Josh was back already with a small plastic carrier in his hand. He gave it to her and she shoved it into her bag without even looking inside.

'Here's the change.'

'Keep it.' She pushed past him. 'I've got to go.'

'I'm coming.'

'Josh . . .'

'I'm coming. You need to tell me about all this. Come on, Sulis. We made a deal.'

She couldn't argue. They left the shop after Josh had looked carefully along the street, and they walked up the hill in silence under his big umbrella. When they turned into the Circus and stopped by the house he was astonished. He gazed up at the windows and whistled. 'You live here?'

She shrugged. 'Just a flat. Look, I can't ask you in now but . . .'

He gazed around at the perfect circle of stone, the ring of acorns that crowned it. Then he said, 'OK. I'll call for you tomorrow. We'll go somewhere. Ten o'clock?'

'Where?' she asked, noticing Hannah peeping though the blind upstairs.

He turned, walking backwards along the pavement, the umbrella dripping round him. 'Wait and see.'

She stood still till he had turned out of the Circus. Then she climbed the steps and groped in her pocket for the key. As she put it in the keyhole, the carved images over the door caught her eye. One was of two hands holding a ring between them. The other was a snake swallowing its tail.

Zac

I confess I loitered by the door trying to look inconspicuous but my striped waistcoat drew plenty of admiring glances.

I'm vain, I know that. It's a failing. And yet Sylvia's mockery galls me. Tonight, as I slipped out of the house past the room where Forrest was working, she had been there, sitting on the stairs, watching. 'Have a good time, Master Peacock,' she had whispered.

A peacock is a stupid, brainless creature. I'm not stupid. Whatever her secrets are, I intend to know all about them.

Gibson's Assembly Rooms for Gentlemen of Taste turned out to be a great florid building all lit with lamps. I entered it between two braziers hot with coals, where sedan-men in livery warmed their hands & a few beggars cadged coins from the drunks who staggered out.

Inside, the rooms were hot & airless, the fug of tobacco & spirits nearly choking me, the salons slightly tawdry

g mirrors. When the flunkey came

party is in the Gilt Room, sir. He asks

tween the tables. Well-dressed men who
ys taking the waters for their gout were
paying ly for it here, smoking & rolling dice or the
ball in the wheel, great piles of coins in front of them.
Spongers & hangers-on urged them to wager. Girls carried
round trays of sweetmeats, their gowns as garish as Sylvia's
had been. They were all painted hussies, their eyes
watchful, assessing each man's wealth.

'This is the room, sir. Thank you, sir.' He eyed the
small coin I had slipped him & bowed coldly, pomade
from his hair dusting my sleeve.

'So you came, Zac.' Lord Compton sat at a card-table
with three other players. He smiled, leaning back. 'I was
sure you would.'

I bowed. The arrogant dog used my name as if I was
his servant. 'How could I resist?'

It was a better room than the others. A crystal chandelier
brilliant with dozens of candles sputtered above. A
sideboard was laden with dishes of cold meats and cheese;
jugs of porter and bottles of fine claret gleamed. Some of
the vintages I recognized from my father's cellar, all sold
now, of course. They were vastly expensive.

Compton wore a robe of some velvet stuff over an
open shirt & black breeches. He'd been drinking but, as

far as I could tell, wasn't drunk. He waved a hand. 'You'll play, Zac.'

It wasn't a request. I didn't move.

'I do not gamble, my lord.' It sounded foolishly stiff, even to me.

'I'm not surprised.' He watched me through the candlelight. A blonde girl came in behind him & leaned over him, draping her arms round his neck. He took no more notice of her than of a fly.

'I gather that's how your father lost his fortune.'

He knew. Did I flinch? Perhaps my hand quivered, because the sword-stick tapped briefly on the floor. I managed to sound calm. 'It's no secret.'

'Gambling is a two-edged sword.' His eyes were blue & clear. 'It lost you everything, but had you never thought to win everything back? This might be the time, & place, Zac.'

'I thought you were offering me a job. If not, I will say goodnight.'

I turned, but he only laughed. 'You are far too proud to be a builder's boy.'

I spun, glaring.

'Or should I say architect's assistant? Either way, it's not much. Especially to a loon like Forrest.'

'Forrest is a genius,' I snarled.

Rather to my surprise, he nodded. 'Maybe. Maybe he is.' He was already dealing the cards & he dealt a hand to me too, his fingers flicking the pasteboard squares expertly. Of his cronies, one was so drunk his head had slumped on his arms & he snored. Another staggered out of the room. The third, a fat, pimply youth, got up & wandered over to the food.

'Leave me out, sirs,' he slurred. 'I am picked clean. Picked clean.'

Lord Compton smiled. He gathered up his cards & looked at them, then at me. 'Play, Zac. You have no fortune left to lose.' His smooth, handsome face had a tiny beauty spot painted below one eye. The foppishness of it annoyed & yet fascinated me. I wondered, briefly, how much it cost to acquire one. Then I peeled off my gloves & picked up the cards.

It was a very good hand.

Compton watched my face. 'Well now. I seem to be a little out of luck. But. . .' He leaned over & slid some coins into the centre of the table. Behind him the door slammed as the fat friend lurched out, the girl giggling with him. In the quiet bright room only the candles hissed & the sleeper snored. I knew this moment was a turning point, a hinge in my life. I could stand up & walk away, or I could draw out that money I had & meet his wager. It was as if a fracture opened in the circle of my life, that there was a gap I could escape through, if I chose.

I looked up, & his smirk infuriated me.

I took out my purse.

An hour later, my coat off, hair tousled where my hands

had run through it, I stared despairingly at the quartet of knaves in my hand & tried to focus on the heap of small papers & coins before me. How much had I lost? How much had I promised him?

The cards blurred; I felt hot, my shirt sticking to the chairback, so I took another sip of the claret. It was sweet & fiery. It made me feel bolder.

Compton had one leg over the chair arm & his head thrown back. He gazed up at the ceiling. 'For God's sake, sir, are you in or out?'

Four knaves. A good hand. The best hand all night. But if I wrote another note …

'How much do I owe you?' My voice was hoarse.

He shrugged. 'Fifty or so.'

Fifty guineas! I didn't have it. I'd never have it. And yet this was my chance to make all even. To win, & get out, & never fall into this wretched folly again. I hated myself with a fierce hatred, & I loathed him, his smirk, his clothes.

I took the pen & wrote. A hundred guineas.

'You will ask your master for it?'

'Of course.' It was a lie & we both knew it. I would never ask Forrest. I could not bear his anger, & his pity.

Compton shrugged. He was lounging so far back that the sumptuous chair teetered on its legs.

'Very well. Let's see your hand. It had better be good, Zac.'

My head was pounding. My mouth felt like chalk. I

placed each one of my knaves down with unsteady fingers, & stared at their triumphant little line. 'There. I believe you cannot beat that, my lord.'

He gazed at me & his eyes were quite clear. 'And what if I can?'

He was bluffing. He had to be. Yet a cold quiver went through me. 'Then I'm finished.'

He nodded. He took one card & laid it down. It was the King of Hearts. 'I am very good at cards, Zac. I have had a great deal of practice.' He laid down the King of Cudgels. 'I spent most of my time at Oxford practising. In truth I have a degree in the subject.' The third card was turned. I sat rigid, watching it. It was the King of Diamonds.

He looked at me over the littered table. The candles had guttered low; drops of hissing wax spatted on the money from the melting masses above.

'Shall I turn the fourth card, Zac? Shall I destroy you?' His hand hovered over the stained pasteboard. 'Or shall I say I have lost, and let you off?'

'You may not have the card.'

'I have it.'

I faced him. His chair was upright now; we were face to face across the circle of light & all the rest of the world was darkness.

I could not help it. My pride scorched me. To lose to him would be unbearable, but to have his pity would leave me nothing of myself. 'I don't believe you,' I said.

He was silent. The noises from the room beyond seemed far & remote. I knew I had angered him. I wanted to. And as he shrugged & flipped the fourth card over I felt nothing for a moment, & then a great exhaustion & a deafness & blindness as if all the world had narrowed to that chequered King of Spades holding its rigid sword.

'So you see, Zac,' he leaned back, 'all your brave talk comes to nothing.'

For a moment then, I really wished to murder him. To snatch out the sword-stick & run him through, flee into the streets & vanish. But I had been seen by too many. I would have to kill myself as well.

'It's an unfair world we live in.' His manicured fingers gathered the money & the notes idly, coin by coin. 'Because, of course, I don't need your pitiable wages. Or the hundred guineas you now owe me.'

I was cleaned out & he knew it. I poured a glass of the claret & drank it off. The wine scorched my aching brain; its warm comfort brought heat to my face. 'My pockets are empty & I have nothing to pay you with.' I tried to sound off-hand; indeed I thrust my fingers into my waistcoat in fuddled scorn & found a small round thing there lodged in the lining, & drew it out.

I tossed it down in disgust. 'Your payment, Sir.'

It was the acorn I had picked up at Stanton Drew. It rolled against the cards & lay still.

Compton didn't laugh. Instead he leaned back & gazed

at me. His scrutiny was hard. He said, 'Perhaps that is a payment I might take.'

'What?'

'The oak is the druids' tree, I believe. Your master has it on his coat-of-arms.'

'Forrest?'

'Forrest.' He leaned forward. 'For my payment, Zac, you can give me Forrest. And I will tear your debts into pieces before your face.'

I sat very still. Then I said, 'I don't understand. What does he have that you don't?'

Compton smiled. His dark hair was still smooth & barely disarrayed, whereas mine was a tragic tangle. He said. 'This new project . . .'

'The Circus.'

'Indeed. It interests me.'

'But you laughed it off! You wouldn't invest . . .'

'Not on his terms. Not to share with him & Alleyn & that fool Greye. But alone, yes, I would build that circle of stone. I would make the world turn & stare at it. Compton's Circus. And when I had built one & made it the height of fashion, I would build others. In London, & Edinburgh, & Newcastle. And the rents I would charge, Zac! All the world would pay through the nose to live there. Because, like you, I recognize a brilliant idea when I see it.'

I could not believe this. My fuddled brain wandered. 'But I don't see what I . . .'

I stopped.

He nodded. 'Yes, you do. Forrest's Circus must fail. The stone must be too costly. The builders must let him down. Men of fashion must snub him.' He sipped from his glass. 'I have already begun that, with talk of his scandalous household. I knew he would take the girl in. He is so easy to predict.'

'You . . . *She works for you?*'

'Let's say dear Sylvia will do anything I tell her to do. With no investors Forrest will be hard pressed for money. He will not be able to afford mistakes. And there will be mistakes, Zac. Small accidents on site. Costly errors.' He raised the glass. 'You'll make sure of that.'

I stood. Or tried to. It was not as dignified as I would have wished. 'He is my master.'

'Oh come. You despise him. Don't you?'

'I have . . . I don't . . .'

'You despise him & this is your chance to be free. He need know nothing. You sabotage the work, he despairs, you suggest selling the design. Then you let me know when he is ready. When all is done, you come & work with me. As my architect. Two young men, out to make their names.' He grinned. 'And your father will be rich again.'

The room reeled.

I had no words. I groped after my coat & sword, & flung them on.

'You don't say no,' he said softly.

For a moment I paused. Then I stumbled to the door, opened it & crashed through, into the smoke & noise of the assembly rooms.

I suppose I walked home. I have no memory of it, or of climbing the stairs. But I must have done, because when I opened my eyes I was sprawled on my bed in my shirt & breeches with a headache that made me gasp. My neck was cricked. I felt as sick as a mongrel after a night in the town dump. The curtains were wide & the sun shone straight in my face. I suppose I must have groaned.

'I'm not surprised,' a voice said coldly.

I managed to turn my head. Forrest & Sylvia stood in the doorway of my room. My master came forward & looked down at me, his arms folded. 'God, Zac, look at the state of you! What sort of assistant am I employing?'

I tried to speak. A crack'd whisper came out.

Forrest sighed. Then he turned to Sylvia. 'I have to go. This morning we begin the transport of the stone. Do what you can to get him presentable.'

He was halfway out before I croaked, 'Wait!'

He turned.

'The stone . . .' My throat was dry; I swallowed. 'Do you mean Ralph Alleyn is still . . .'

'Master Alleyn is my true friend. He is selling me the stone & his waggons will begin bringing it down the hill today.' Forrest's dark eyes watched me; I noticed he was dressed for work in his oldest brown coat. 'I told you I will build the Circus, Zac, & I intend to do it. Now please, get yourself to a decent state & attend me on the site. I shall have things to say to you.'

He glanced at Sylvia, then walked out. I heard him running down the wooden stairs & out into the street.

I closed my eyes. In the darkness in my head bright bands of pain flashed & stabbed like knives in a dungeon. I wanted to curl up & die.

After a while the girl's voice said, 'Drink this.'

I refused to move.

'I said drink, Master Peacock. Or crawl outside & be sick. It's one or the other.'

I ungummed my eyes. She was holding a pewter tankard, & I was appalled. 'Never. Never again.'

'It's not wine. It will do you good. We all used it at Gibson's.'

She was actually sitting on my bed. I forced myself to sit up. 'I don't need your help.' It was so weak a lie I was not surprised at her laughter. So I snatched the beaker from her & drank.

'*God!*' It was minutes before I could speak. 'What utter bilge is that!'

Sylvia hugged her knees where she sat. 'I won't tell you. You'd vomit.'

'Then don't.' I was shivering. I clutched the sheets about me.

'Finish it.'

She obviously thought I couldn't, so I did. It was

totally, absolutely foul. Then I lay back & let the room swim in & out of my head.

'You went to see Compton.'

I didn't move. But her accusation came through the mist like a sudden stab of light.

'I could have told you not to go. He's filth, that one.'

I opened my eyes. She was watching me with that coy look I had begun to recognize. Her face was a little fuller, as if only a few days of good food had begun to change her. Some of the poxy spots had faded. I said, 'How did you know?'

'You're not the only one who reads notes from other people's pockets.'

I sat bolt upright, the pain forgotten.

'Oh yes. I know all about how you spy on your master.' Her eyes were a scornful blaze. 'What did Compton want? Has he got his claws in you?'

I had no intention of telling her anything. But I felt so sick I had to speak. 'We played cards. I ended up owing him money.'

'How much?'

'More than I can ever pay. A hundred guineas.'

Her eyes widened. We shared a terrified moment, & then I managed a shrug. 'Well, I must find the money.'

'Tell Forrest.'

'No!' My voice was sharp. 'Never.'

She rose with a rustle of the silk dress & went to the window & opened it. Cold air gusted in, with a whistle of birdsong. I hastily curled in the bedclothes.

After a moment she said, 'He ensnared you. Because he sees you & Forrest, how you are together. And he thinks, "This one will get me what I want." And what is that, Zac? What is it he wants?'

In the darkness of the blankets I could not answer her. Instead I said, 'Compton said I despised Forrest.'

She laughed. 'So you do, Zac Peacock . . .'

'Stop calling me that!'

'Why? It's true.' She came & pulled the blanket off my face, & I saw she was pale with anger. 'Take a good look at yourself. A wastrel – lazy & vain & sure the world owes him his fortune! Yet you *dare* to look down on Jonathan Forrest, a man worth ten of you.'

'I do not. I respect Forrest . . .'

'Then show it.' She swept to the door & turned there. 'You owe him everything just as I do. Why do you think he employs you? For your skill? You have none! Because your father pays him? Nothing is paid for you, Zac, not a farthing! Cook told me no one else in the city would take any apprentice for free, let alone pay him a wage. But Master Forrest takes in waifs & strays bcause he is a man of generosity & he knows what it is to be despised. A genius is never loved. Even when his desire is only to create beauty.' She gripped the door handle & took a breath. In a quieter voice she said, 'Whatever it is Compton wants you to do, be careful. The fine lord is a gutter rat.'

'You'd know.'

I had managed to sit on the side of the bed. The room was still queasy, but I saw how she looked at me then, her glance as quick & fierce as a vixen's. We were both silent. For a moment I knew I could have spat back venom at her too, taunted her that she was Compton's creature, as much a traitor as I. I don't know why I said nothing.

She pushed back a wisp of hair. 'Get up. Work begins today. We have to help him, Zac. The Circus is more than a building. It will be the perfection of his work.'

'What is his work to you? Who are you anyway? Is Sylvia even your real name?'

She and I eyed each other. Then, she said, 'If I tell you, you will despise me.'

'No.'

'I think so.'

'Try me.'

For a moment I thought she would. Then Mrs Hall called & she cried, 'Coming!' She turned & without looking at me said, 'Maybe tomorrow.'

When she had gone I was left alone in the cold sunshine with my raging head. And her rose scent. And my rankling self-disgust.

Bladud

It is a strange thing to have been an outcast and now to be a king again. I looked at the land with new eyes. I saw its shapes and curves, that places in it were powerful and others were accursed.

As if the gods had left their footprints behind them.

I watched the people. They came from far away, beyond the horizon. They came on foot, carried on waggons, high on horses. They came with every sickness and disease, the blind, the foolish, the broken-limbed, the elf-stricken.

All of them sought the healing of Sulis.

For a time, I feared the spring would fail us. In hot weather I was sure it would dry up. But she never betrayed us. And so the people scrubbed themselves in the hot spring; they drank the sulphurous water.

They made statues of her, of branches and flowers, then of wood, then of stone.

But I was not content. I had been touched by magic, and I had to pay her back. I wanted to inscribe my joy on the world. So I made circles. On the downs we made one that was vast and powerful, ring within ring within ring. I set an acorn in that ground too, that would one day be a great tree. And all around the spring, I built her a city, of fine houses, and a temple for her image, so that the bramble valley was a shining place. I lit a fire for her that would never go out.

Sulis

She was worried about Josh coming to the house and Hannah must have noticed, because after breakfast she said, 'Everything OK?'

'Fine, thanks.'

'I've got a day off too. We could go shopping if you like.'

Sulis frowned. She was curled up on the window seat in the sunny sitting room flicking through one of Simon's books on the city. An illustration caught her eye; she turned the pages back to find it. 'I can't. I mean I'd like to, another day, but a friend's calling for me. Any minute.'

'Anyone I know?'

'Josh. He works at the museum.' The questions were intrusive but she tried not to get annoyed. Instead she found the page and smoothed it open. It showed a painting of three men in eighteenth-century coats and breeches gathered round a table; a stiff, formal group looking directly out at the viewer. Before them lay an artful scatter of pens, scrolls, surveying instruments, a model of the sun and moon. And a large unrolled plan of the Circus, overlaid with a triangle and some other strange symbols. One of the men had his forefinger touching the paper, pointing at the empty centre of the Circus. Was he Jonathan Forrest?

A shadow on the page made her glance up. Hannah was turning a mug of tea in anxious hands; her hair was untidier than ever. She blew a wisp of it out of her eyes. 'I don't want to pry, Su, you know that, but . . . well when you say friend, do you mean like, a boyfriend?'

Sulis tried not to cringe. She kept her eyes on the page. 'No, I don't. Just because he's a boy . . .'

'I know! Believe me, I hate asking. It's just . . . well, you know. The situation.'

Simon came in then. 'What about the situation?'

'Sulis has made a new friend. Josh. He's coming round.'

The room was silent. Sulis realized her teeth were gritted with tension; she relaxed and glanced up at Simon. The whole thing was ridiculous. 'If you want I'll call it off. It's not that important . . .'

Simon had an armful of files and drawings. He put them down carefully on the table. 'Maybe we need to discuss this a bit.'

'Why? You said live a normal life . . .'

'But you should have mentioned him, Sulis. I don't want to be heavy, but we have to be very careful.'

'He doesn't know anything about the past. He's my age. Do I have to tell you about everyone I ever talk to?'

She knew she sounded defensive; her voice had risen to a whiny, stupidly high note.

Simon sat down on the seat next to her. 'Of course not.'

'Good.' To break the awkwardness she hefted the heavy book to face him. 'Look. Is that Forrest?'

Simon glanced at Hannah. Then he took the book and looked at it and she sensed that he was being especially patient, his whole pose a considering caution. 'Yes. That's him. I believe it's the only known image of what he looked like. You see he's pointing to the centre of the Circus? There's a story that he wanted some sort of secret feature there, but whatever it was was never completed. There was just a reservoir for water; you can see the roof of it out there, between the trees.'

She glanced out. The ground between the planes was thick with golden leaves.

Simon followed her gaze. 'Well maybe not now. In summer. This man here in red was Ralph Alleyn, a local bigwig who owned the stone quarries. Pretty rich.'

'And him?' She pointed to the boy at Forrest's side.

'Zachariah Stoke. Forrest's assistant. Can't remember what happened to him. But look, Sulis, are you sure this Josh knows nothing about you?'

'He knows you're my parents. We live here. I'm going to uni next year. That's it. End of story.'

She was used to lying but she didn't like lying to them. They were so innocent somehow. As if she was older than them. Generations older. And in a way she was, because she had seen death and evil close up, and they never had.

Simon looked at Hannah. She said brightly, 'Well I'm sure it will be all right. Where are you going?'

'I don't know. It's up to him.' Sulis turned back to the book. She sensed Hannah's jerk of the head to Simon; they both went out into the kitchen and after a while the murmurs of their conversation drifted in.

Sulis stared hard at the painting, as if it could stop her hearing them. Zachariah Stoke looked about her age. He had a haughty, self-confident air, his head slightly on one side, as if he was listening to somebody too, in that distant room. Perhaps it had been a room in the Circus. Maybe even this one. He was handsome, and rather fine, but it was Forrest who interested her. The architect had a face full of energy, of fierce enthusiasm. He gazed out at her as if he challenged her; as if there was something she and he could share. Perhaps, she thought, it was that each of them had only one image that the world could see. One picture that would define them for ever. 'So this is how they caught you,' she whispered. There was a sadness about him too, as if all the things he loved had failed him.

The doorbell rang.

Sulis looked up. She felt a sudden pang of nerves and

that annoyed her. Josh was early.

'I'll go.' Hannah came out of the kitchen. 'Are you OK about him coming up?'

'He'll have to. I'm not ready.' She put the book down and hurried upstairs.

As she found her coat and money she heard voices below; when she ran down Josh was standing by the window talking to Simon politely about the view.

'It's a bit like a clock,' Josh was saying. 'A stone clock.'

'Well yes. The sun travels round it. The shadows of the trees are like dark pointers.' Simon sounded impressed. 'Are you a student?'

'I was. Not now.' That tense note had come into Josh's voice.

'Architecture?'

'Archaelogy.'

'Really? Well if you're interested, there's a project about to begin here in the Circus that you might help me out with. I can't promise money . . .'

Sulis said, 'You never told me that.'

Simon turned. 'Oh well I was going to, of course. It's not exactly glamorous. A new storm drain is due to be laid across the green down there – it will run from roughly our cellar to the other side, so I've pulled a few strings and the contractors have offered the university the chance to work there if anything turns up.'

Josh said, 'What sort of things?'

'Who knows?' Simon smiled his lecturer's smile. 'If you're interested . . .'

Sulis was annoyed. 'I'm interested.'

'Oh, I meant both of you, of course.'

Hannah was clearing the breakfast table. 'Just like a man.'

Sulis moved to the door. She had to get Josh out of here. 'I need to get my phone.' She pulled his sleeve. 'Come on. I'll show you the view from the roof.'

In her bedroom she opened the window and he stepped through and whistled. 'This is amazing. Have you ever worked your way along the roof?'

'No. And don't you.'

He put his arms round the stone acorn. 'These things look smaller from below. Why acorns, anyway?'

'Bladud's crown, so Simon says.' She grinned. '*Simon says*.'

Josh even laughed. He seemed different today, up here. Less self-absorbed. Happier. Above him the sky was blue and clear and cold. It was as if they had risen above their lives and, for a moment, were free.

A voice echoed, strangely distorted. It spoke garbled, harsh syllables. *A ripple*, it said, *in the pool of time*.

'What's that?' Josh turned.

She sighed. 'The tourist bus.'

It came around the corner, as it did every hour, the red double-decker slowly purring round the circular road.

126

'Do they look in through your windows?' Josh grinned.

'Sometimes.'

The commentary drifted across to them, the woman with the microphone muffled in hat and scarf, her voice rebounding from the opposite houses.

'. . . Jonathan Forrest's masterpiece, built to a complex and secret theory. Thirty houses in three sections, using the three orders of architecture. Begun in 1740, Forrest's survey of Stonehenge inspired his . . .'

The bus came round towards them, scattering jackdaws into the trees. There were a few people downstairs, all foreign tourists, but on the upper, open deck, there was only one man. He was sitting on the back seat, muffled against the cold in a coat and a scarf wrapped tightly round his neck. Sulis stared at him.

Was it?

Dread paralyzed her. Josh was talking, but she couldn't even hear him.

The man had dark hair. He was gazing at the houses he passed intently, with a fixed fascination, and yet he was doing something too, dialling a number into a mobile phone he held.

'Sulis?'

Josh had had to stand directly in front of her. 'Am I that boring?'

'It's him.' She pushed him aside, and he wobbled and grabbed hastily at the acorn.

'Be careful!'

'It's him. I know it. There, *look*!' She grabbed him, turned him. 'At the back, on his own.'

He stared. The bus drew slowly level with them. The man raised his eyes and gazed calmly across at them.

'. . . please note the mysterious frieze of images above the columns,' the microphone droned. 'Symbols of occult and unknown imagery, as if Forrest was leaving a message for later generations, never deciphered . . .

The man smiled at her.

Sulis couldn't move. She stared at him and he gazed back, and she was on the top of the tower in her red coat and Caitlin was standing too near the edge, sidling towards it one foot at a time saying, 'It's OK. It's quite safe, look.' But then Caitlin was a boy and he was saying, 'Are you sure it's the same man? I don't think it is.'

'Sure. Utterly sure. I dream about him.'

The man lifted the mobile to his ear. He leaned back on the seat, gazing at her.

Her phone rang.

The shock was so great she dropped it. It fell with a clatter on to the narrow stone ledge and skittered to the edge. The vibrations of its ringtone made it shudder in a tiny circle.

Josh crouched. 'I can get it.'

'No! Don't!'

'I can reach it.' His fingers groped. 'It's just . . .'

He leaned further.

128

'Don't!'

'It's OK. It's safe. Look.'

She stood behind him and the wind blew and the birds cawed and flew around her. The man's eyes were fixed on her and she was sick and shivering and she had hold of his coat and was pulling and she wanted to scream but the words were choked in her throat.

Josh's fingers closed on the phone. He scrabbled it nearer. 'If I can just . . .' He was over the empty, sheer edge of the roof.

'Caitlin,' she breathed. 'Don't . . .'

He squirmed back. He scrambled up. 'Who's Caitlin?'

'She's dead,' she whispered.

Awkward, he handed her the phone. 'You should answer this.'

'No. No one knows this number. No one but Hannah and Simon.'

He held it out to her but she couldn't take it. The bus had passed them; it was turning out of the Circus and through the windscreen at the back she could still see the man sitting there. He didn't turn his head.

'Hello?' Josh had the phone to his ear, looking at her. 'Who is this?'

She knew who it was.

Intent, she watched Josh's face as the jackdaws came down in a squawking cloud on the roofs and the trees.

For a minute he was expressionless. Then he pushed the button and gave the phone back to her. 'No answer.'

She looked at the tiny screen. It said NUMBER UNOBTAINABLE. She felt giddy. For an instant she felt how the whole world was spinning round the sun, in a circle so fast no one even noticed. She took a step sideways and bumped against the acorn. The sun was blinding her eyes.

She didn't remember how they got inside. She was sitting on the bed and Josh was propped on the chair. He was looking at her.

They were both silent.

For a moment there was only silence, and then he said, 'We should go out.'

'No! We'll stay here.' She swallowed. 'I'll tell you here.'

There was no sound from below. Simon would have gone to work and if Hannah had shouted up to say she was going out neither of them would have heard her. The small room was quiet and warm and the sunlight streamed in.

Josh took his coat off and tossed it down. 'I could murder a cup of tea.'

She had to talk. She said, 'That photo. On the book cover.'

She leaned over and pulled a drawer open and tossed the book on to the bed. They both stared at it. Josh didn't touch it. He said, 'This Caitlin . . .'

'She's in it too.'

He leaned back. He took a small wooden clown that

130

was on her table and pulled the string that made it collapse. But he didn't say anything.

And suddenly the silence yawned, and she knew only her words could fill it.

'Sulis is not my real name. I was born in Sheffield, and I lived there until I was seven with my mum . . . not Hannah, my real mum. We had a house on an estate, just outside the town. A bit small, a bit . . . scruffy. I didn't think so then, but I suppose I do now.'

She curled up on the bed, as if she was telling herself the story. And it was easy to tell, because she had rehearsed it over and over for this moment. The moment she would explain.

'It was just an ordinary life and I was just an ordinary kid. I didn't have a dad, but that's true for a lot of people. We didn't have any family though. My mum never talked about them that I remember.

'I went to the local primary school and I must have been in the reception class when I met Caitlin. I don't remember a time in school when she wasn't there. She sat by me a lot. There was a whole class of kids but she was my friend. You know, the way little girls are. My special friend.'

He collapsed the toy again, and nodded. She sensed he didn't want to interrupt her.

'She was . . . funny. And chatty. A bit loud. She was always doing things and saying things . . . If there was something going on . . . I don't know, a fight or an argument, she was in it. She was always pulling me after her. I followed her. She was stronger than me. I sort of knew that.' She curled up, tighter. 'Other people didn't like her. My mother started to say, 'That Caitlin . . .' The teacher split us up but we always played together in the yard. She wasn't supposed to come to my house. So I only saw her then in school. We were ordinary little kids. We got into trouble, but only silly things. We would have grown up to be just ordinary teenage girls, I suppose. If that day hadn't happened.'

Josh was listening, his fingers on the toy. She said, 'It was a cold morning. Sunny, but cold. It must have been autumn . . . Just after the schools go back, because we had a new teacher, and she didn't like Caitlin. There was some trouble, I forget what, a row with some girl. Caitlin got the blame, and then she lost her temper, and punched the other kid. She'd had to go to the head teacher's office, and her mum was going to get a letter about it. She was really upset. We were in a corner of the playground that lunchtime and she was there with her back against the wire fence and her face all red from crying and her knees up and she was so wild. *I'm not staying here to get yelled at again*, she said. *I'm going. Are you coming?*

'I don't think I wanted to. I wouldn't have done it on my own. But she was like that. You had to go along. She sort of pulled you after her.

'We crept past the dinner ladies and round by the

staff car park. There was a wall but it was easy to get over. I remember we were two streets away, running down an alley, when I heard the bell go for the afternoon, and thinking that I'd miss PE and that I was quite pleased about that.'

She looked up. 'Sorry. All this . . .'

'I'm interested. Go on.'

He had dumped the toy. Now he wasn't fiddling with anything, his eyes on her.

She looked away. 'We'd never been out on our own before. At least I hadn't. We knew a few streets but after that it was all new. Cars and a zebra crossing and then a bus stop. A bus came and Caitlin said *Let's get on it* so we did. We didn't have any money, but there was a crowd of women and we got on with them and sat together, all innocent, and I suppose everyone thought we were someone else's kids. The bus went through the countryside for miles – woods and fields and then into another town and we got off and ran. We didn't care. Not yet. We walked down streets and found this big park, so we played on the swings – and then we ran around a little lake that was there. It was fun at first. I don't know how long it took us to realize that we were lost, and it was cold, and we were hungry.' She looked up. 'People tell kids not to talk to strangers, but everyone is a stranger, nearly, and all of a sudden we realized that. There were no friendly firemen or policemen or women in nurses' uniforms like in the pictures in kids' reading books, no kind old ladies walking dogs. It was twilight and the tree branches were black against the sky and the streetlamps were all orange. I remember that. It was getting dark. And I remember how the birds scared me – flocks of birds swooping into the trees, squawking.

'Then we saw him.

'He was sitting on a bench in the park.

'He looked all right. I think he was watching the birds or maybe I've imagined that. It's so hard to tell what you remember from what you imagine. Or what other people whisper around you. And I've read all the cuttings now, of course, so there's all that newspaper stuff in my head too.'

'You spoke to him?'

'Caitlin did. She was always the bravest. I stayed back. I don't know what she said but he stood up and walked over to us. He seemed really tall, but he sort of crouched down. And close up he was all dirty. I mean stinking. And we saw that his clothes were old and he had some sort of disease . . . well, that's what I thought. It was probably just sores, but anyway we screamed, and ran.'

She was silent so long Josh heard the tourist bus go round again on its endless cycle. When she spoke again her voice was quieter. 'He chased us. Over the grass, up some sort of slope. We were terrified. He shouted but we didn't stop. Then there was a sort of building in front of us. A tall, round building. It had a door, and we opened it and fell inside and shoved the door shut and sat there in the dark, all huddled up together, all panting and breathless and scared absolutely stiff. We thought he was coming after us. It took ages for us to stop sobbing and shaking and to think we were safe. Finally Caitlin whispered that we should go back outside. I didn't want to but she made me. So we tried to open the door. But we couldn't.'

'It was locked?'

'Jammed, I suppose. It was a big old wooden door. We could barely reach the handle, let alone turn it. We banged and yelled and screamed. We forgot the man could still be out there. We didn't care – all I wanted was my mum, and to be safe and home and warm. But no one came.'

Josh shook his head. 'It must have been bad.'

'We were seven years old. We thought we'd die in there. I was sure I'd never see my house or my toys or my school again. And in a sense I was right, because nothing was ever the same after.' She rolled over and sat up, pushing her hair back. 'Anyway, after a while Caitlin had an idea. *Let's go up the steps*, she said. *There might be a window*. So we climbed up. The steps were wet and slippery, and they curved round. Like steps in a castle – one of my foster-parents took me to a castle once and I nearly fainted. I couldn't go up there. The dark, the damp smell, the slime on the walls – it was just the same.

'Our breath sounded really loud, and it was dark and

there were cobwebs and horrible spiders. But no windows. We climbed up and up until our legs hurt, and there was another door and it was stiff, but we managed to push that one open, and there was a room. Empty, except for some old sacks and rubbish in one corner. In the wall was a tiny gate, of iron, sort of like a portcullis, and there was a wind coming through it, so we ran over and pulled and tugged at it. It was all white with bird mess. But we opened it, and the wind whipped in.

'Outside was the roof. A little flat square of roof, with a broken parapet. In the newspapers after they called it a folly. A folly.' She smiled, shaking her head. 'What a joke.'

Josh was very still. 'Sulis. You don't have to . . .'

'I want to tell you. I've got this far, and I don't want you to read it in some trashy book. I want you to know what really happened.' She had to keep talking. If she stopped she might never come this far again, and she had to know, she herself, had to know what had happened.

Because this was a story she never let herself remember to its end, except where she had no control over it, in dreams, where it swelled into grotesque faces and garbled words. She spoke quickly now, in a rapid monotone.

'We didn't know what to do. We were so high up and down below was the park, and the lake, and it was all so dark and quiet. The trees and bushes were black; they

136

were like some forest in a fairy tale, a place where witches are. There was no one to hear us even if we'd shouted. And then it started to rain, an icy sleet, and we were sobbing so hard.' She shook her head, and cleared her throat.

'People must have missed you.'

'Oh they had. When neither of us came home from school there was a while when each of our mothers was just annoyed, and then they panicked. By about five the police were called, and they started to search. But it was a freezing night, and what no one realized was just how far we'd come. It was that bus ride. It turned out after that we were about ten miles from home. So everyone was looking in the wrong place.'

'What did you do?'

'We just stood there.'

'And then?'

She was silent a moment. Then she said, 'He came. The tramp. We heard him behind us. He'd come up the stairs, I suppose. He ducked under the metal grille. He said, *There's no way down from here, little girls. Unless you can fly.*

Zac

Alleyn's rail waggons are a wonder. The stone is brought down from the quarries in them, on a steep wooden track right down to the river, powered by nothing but gravity. The shouts of men & haulers can be heard across the city. At the quay the rough blocks are manhandled into a line of waggons that rumbles constantly through the streets & up here to the site. I have never seen such industry. It astonishes & rather shames me.

The labourers are low creatures from the nearby farms & villages but they work harder than beasts. It is as if the work is the deepest thing in them, this hauling of stones, heaving of stones, shaping & chiselling & cutting of stones. Perhaps they are the descendents of the ancient fellows who built Stone-henge. Forrest would say, so, I'm sure.

It is a pity their industry will be subverted by me.

I have a small shelter here on site in which to work. Of course, we are not builders. We are architects & gentlemen, we. The building contractors are men as rough as their workers, each responsible for a number of houses. They fit out the insides as their buyers wish, those that are sold. What we oversee is more important. The facade. The very shape of the Circus.

I have a bench & stool & a small fire in a brazier to keep my feet warm, though the weather is still mild. I have a flask of wine in the drawer. Sipping it, I watched the labourers & thought of Sylvia. Yesterday, she told me her story.

She told it falteringly in broken sentences. I said little, because I would not have her stop. And yet there were many things she did not say. I knew her name was false, & she admitted that, but never once did she say what her real name was. And this village in the north may not even exist. But her running away with a friend, & their adventuring here to Aquae Sulis, & her fall into the vices & gamblings of Gilbert's, why this is an old tale. She lost all her money, & had to work for her keep, & until Forrest rescued her she was lower than the sweepings of the street.

She denies passionately that she works for Compton now. She loathes him, & rarely goes out in case she meets with him, or any of the wastrels of the city. And certainly my lord is a liar. But I wonder if she, like me, is his instrument to destroy the success of the Circus, even if she does not know it? Her very presence in the house damages Forrest.

Forrest was out on site, his plans spread on a table in the windy air. I watched him pointing & gesturing & giving careful orders.

He cannot be in love with her, can he? He is old enough to be her father.

Can it just be kindness?

Such a simple thing?

George Fisher came in, a carpenter. 'The mazter wants ee.' They do not even call me 'Zirr' these days. I got up, dusted my clothes, & went.

The site was a maelstrom of noise. Chipping, hammering, the teeth-gritting scrape of metal on stone. Dust blew in my face & nostrils, despite my handkerchief. Forrest turned as I came.

'Zac. Morris reports more despoilation overnight. Tools taken, a wooden cradle burnt.'

I looked suitably dismayed. But I thought, *This is why Compton needs me, To create his chaos.*

'What about the night-watchmen?'

'They saw nothing. Between you & me, I fear they are paid to see nothing.' He clouted the table with his fist & I saw the anger in him. 'Why do they do this to me? Don't they see the wonder of this place? The beauty of the shape?'

'Perhaps they hear rumours of games & gladiators.' I felt guilty. Perhaps that was why my voice came out silky & needle-sharp.

He glared.

'All that is forgotten & you know it. I have had enough of mockery from Lord Compton without you repeating it. And I cannot afford this, Zac. I am mortally short of money.'

He looks tired. There are dark smudges under his eyes. For two nights he has worked, & yet late last night, deep in the dark hours, he left the house with two strangers & did not come home before dawn. More of the Oroboros mystery.

I said, 'We could economize.'

'I will not. This structure will stand long after both of us are dead, & I will not be thought a scrapeshift.'

I shrugged. 'The stone columns must be kept, yes, but there are aspects of the design that you could omit without spoiling it. The stone acorns, for example. They have no purpose. I am not sure if they won't even mar the purity of the thing. And then there are these metopes . . .'

He gave a great swearing oath & stormed up and down, ignoring the workmen's stares.

'The metopes are part of the whole! The acorns matter! I will not compromise, sir, even if I have to sell everything I own.'

These metopes are strange things, mere emblems & pictures in stone. He has selected some from foreign books & others he has drawn himself. They are alchemical signs, secret devices. A Janus face – both male & female. An oak tree. Beehives. Two hands breaking a ring. The frieze of them will carry right around the circle, but what

141

will the buyers of the houses want with such images on their property? *And acorns?*

I stepped back from his wrath & said icily, 'Well, sir, perhaps you could ask help from your secret friends.'

He stopped. Sometimes he is like a puppet glove on my hand. I know exactly what he will say.

'What secret friends?'

'The Oroboros Society. Or whatever they call themselves.'

Or do I know him? He stared at me so long I was almost afraid, & then he smiled. In all the clamour of stonecutting & rattle of waggons there was silence between us.

'Well, Zac. You watch carefully.'

I felt awkward. 'I saw them at Stanton Drew, as you know. I know there are many such secret orders. Masons, druidical societies, clubs of learned men.'

His dark eyes still held me. 'Then you will know their members cannot discuss their secrets.'

'Well indeed, sir, but I am sure if a member is in need of help – of any sort – his co-druids, or whatever they are, would assist him.' It struck me then that the emblems on the frieze were symbols of this group, so I kept silent. When he spoke again he amaz'd me.

He said, 'You are good to think of my welfare, Zac. I appreciate it.'

'I! But I . . .'

'Oh you may keep up your haughty ways, but I see the

real you. You hurt me to the quick by suggesting I cut the acorns from my plan & now you seek to offer comfort.' He came up to me & put both his hands on my shoulders. 'You are loyal, Zac, & despite your roistering I know you dream of the Circus as I do. We'll get through this trouble. The Circus will be your memorial as well as mine.'

One of the men called him then & he went. I stared at his back. He had not been sarcastic. He did not know the meaning of the word! For a while I stood there in the clamour & then I turned & walked furiously off the site. Why did he have to say that? *Loyalty?* What did he know of my loyalty? I was loyal to no man but myself.

I walked down to the town & shame & anger fuelled me. The debt to Compton felt like a load on my back. A hundred guineas! In truth it might as well have been a thousand – I was ruined & I knew it.

But as I strode through the filth of the narrow alleys it was Forrest I was angry with. He might be a genius but surely no man could be so simple. So stupid! And after all, I owed him nothing. Sylvia's scornful words were a girl's folly. Anyone would have taken me on as apprentice, fee or not! I was educated, the son of a gentleman. Architects everywhere would have jumped at the chance.

I would not care about Forrest. He was kind only when it suited him & star-blind with his own obsessions. His druidical nonsense was making fools of us all.

I came out into the Abbey churchyard. To my right the

great Gothic building rose, its blackened facade showing the double ladders of stone that led up to heaven, angels climbing them. To catch my breath I stopped & stared up at it.

Whoever had designed this had also been a man of genius, but who remembered him now? Ladies & gentlemen strolled beneath the fan vaulting & great windows & marvelled at the stonework. They never once thought of the builders. Stones remain, men die. This is how things are. This is what the circle means.

'Good day, Master Stoke.'

I turned, quickly.

Two men & a lady stood there. She wore a red silk dress that must have cost the earth. One of the men was Ralph Alleyn.

'Master Alleyn,' I said.

'Allow me to introduce Sir John Douglas. Lady Douglas. This is my friend Forrest's assistant, Master Zachariah Stoke.'

We all bowed elegantly. *Forrest's assistant*, I thought. No more than this.

'You must be busy at the site.' Alleyn came & took my arm & we all walked towards the baths.

'Since the ground was levelled things have moved quickly. The first third of the facade is begun.'

'John will build in sections?'

'That's the idea.'

He nodded & stood elegantly posed in the sunlight. I

heard the swish of his brocade coat, & I thought, *He is rich. Try him.*

I said, 'Things are not right, sir. There have been thefts, deliberate destructions. Small, but troublesome.'

He frowned, waving his friends on. I saw them sweep into the Abbey.

'So I've heard. But it will be nothing, Zac. There are always thefts from sites. John knows that.' He shook his head so that the fine silvery wig shed a little powder. 'I'll call on him. There are no problems with the stone, I trust?'

'The stone is perfect.' I took a breath. 'Master Alleyn, if I may . . . it's just . . . on my own account I have . . . a little difficulty.'

I did not like the look he gave me. It was direct & his eyes were hard. 'Difficulty?'

I laughed, a feeble attempt. 'Money, sir. You know how a gentlemen has . . . obligations. I wonder if I might possibly impose . . .'

He caught my sleeve & hauled me into the shelter of the bathhouse. From over the wall the splashes of the hot water & howls of the afflicted rose like catcalls. He said, 'Don't speak to me as if we were in some book of etiquette, sir. Do you mean to tell me that you have been gambling & are in debt?'

I pulled away. I had never heard him so sharp. I raised my chin. 'Once. Just once. Unfortunately I . . .'

'How much?'

'Sir?'

'Don't pretend to be stupid, boy. How much do you owe?'

I opened my mouth but the words came out in a sullen mutter. 'A hundred. Guineas.'

I had thought him such a soft man. Now I saw I was wrong. He fixed me with a look that could shatter stone.

'I warned John not to take you on, did you know that? But he laughed & said, 'Oh come, let's give the boy a chance, Ralph.' And this is how you repay him! I tell you, sir, you fill me with disgust. He works himself to the bone & his genius is scorned by fools & even his own apprentice is a scoundrel. If I hear money is missing from his house I shall . . .'

I jerked back. 'I would never do that! Never!'

'I think you might do much.'

We glared at each other. Passers-by turned their heads, curious. Alleyn said, 'Whom do you owe?'

'I can't tell you that.' I wouldn't. I was hot with fury. 'Forget I asked you. I'll find the money myself.'

'Does John know?'

'No. You will not tell him, sir.'

'I will not tell him *yet*. And I will give you this.' He scribbled something on a card & held it out to me. 'The address of a reputable man of business. No villain. He will lend you the money for a reasonable amount of interest on my backing.' He pushed it into my hand. 'But I swear, Zac, I will never do this again. And I don't do it

146

for you, but for my good friend, who has the misfortune to be kind to ungrateful strays.'

He did not bow.

He just turned & walked away.

I stood grasping my sword-stick in the middle of the square, the paper crushed in my glove. My face burned. I was sure everyone was staring at me but I couldn't move.

Sheer raw fury made my hands tremble.

After a moment I raised my head & walked with exaggerated poise to the wall & gazed over at the bathers. I barely saw them. The steam of the hot springs rose into the autumn air, & I stared at the fat women & the gouty men as if I would kill them all. What sort of a world was this? And there in the open bath, beggars & low women & poxed fools all squatting together in who knows what filth, hoping for a cure for diseases they had brought down upon themselves, & richly deserved. I hated all of them.

I hated the whole world.

How could I ever pay interest! Couldn't he see I was desperate? I narrowed my eyes & swore softly & in that instant I knew what I would do. I glanced at the name on the paper, crushed it & flung it into the hot bath. Let Sulis have it, as an offering. I turned. Walking quickly, I slipped into the alleys. And then I ran.

Up the slope of the town. Past leaning houses & building sites for new smart terraces. Past shops & gaming halls & assembly rooms & market stalls. Through the tumbledown tangle of the old & the graceful streets of the new, past sedan chairs and phaetons, through black iron railings, by maids scrubbing the steps, & split beer from a dray & two cockerels fighting in the road.

I ran home to Forrest's house & opened the door & slipped in & listened.

From the kitchen Mrs Hall's voice droned. She must be talking to Sylvia. I crept up the stairs & slid into Forrest's workroom & closed the door without a sound. Careful on the creaking boards, I slipped off my shoes & padded past the great model of the Circus. For a moment, just a fierce, hot moment, I was tempted to smash it all to splinters, but that would be nothing. I would do something much worse than that. I would see that debt torn up in front of my eyes & pay back Forerest's patronizing kindness & his foppish friend who had dared to look down on me.

His desk was littered with papers. Plans, diagrams, notes for a new manuscript. Books of geometry & alchemy. Tools & string & pens & ink.

I found the master designs for the Circus. Lighting the lamp, I glanced up at the skylight & saw that the short afternoon was already waning. It would be dark soon – I had little time. Choosing a pen I sat down & pulled the plans towards me.

I made a copy. But not a perfect one.

The changes would be tiny, & no one would notice

them. Measurements a few inches out, columns a little too far to the left. Door-cases misaligned. Small things. Maybe not even Forrest would notice them until they were done, but they would be there, & if they were built they would destroy the harmony & perfection of the Circus.

I nodded, grimly, as my pen dipped in the ink. Proportion was everything. That was the magic, & I would skew it. And always, for ever after, the eye of the onlooker would not be pleased but wander restlessly round the circle of houses, unable to find out what was wrong. What was lopsided, what was out of place.

I would leave my own mark on the world. Like a dark angel, I would bring discord into paradise. And let Forrest & Compton & Alleyn and all of them go hang themselves!

I worked for an hour. When at last I sat up & gazed around, the night had come.

The room was dark beyond the pool of light on the desk.

The last thing I did was redraw one of the metopes. Instead of the tree standing tall, I drew it fallen, shattered by lightning.

Later, in my own garret I lay on the bed & listened to the sounds of the house, Forrest coming in, his shout, Sylvia's call of welcome. Outside my window jackdaws karked & laughed. I remembered the birds trapped in that unfinished room, how they had flung themselves so foolishly at the windows, how they had broken their own necks out of panic & fear & mindlessness.

All at once I felt a terrible dread that I had done the same.

Or fallen, from some great height.

Bladud

To build a masterpiece, a man must first learn about the earth. He must discover the secrets of how to enclose space, because this controls the behaviour of people. Birds are free, they live in the limitless air, but men are ruled by walls and corridors and streets and roads. If these are in harmony, so will the people be.

The architect is a magician, and a king.

So I travelled and studied. I saw Troy and Jerusalem and Avalon.

I bowed before Apollo.

I measured the temple of Solomon.

I sailed beyond the North Wind.

And always I searched for the perfect shape, the knowledge and power of its proportions.

Because I was determined to build the greatest building in all Logria.

A building that would be known for ever.

A ripple in the pool of time.

Sulis

The kettle boiled and rattled and clicked itself off. Josh lifted it and poured the steaming water into a teapot. He stirred it and put it on the tray with the sugar and the two striped mugs and carried everything carefully into the room. 'Your kitchen is crazy.'

Sulis nodded. 'That's Hannah. She's into herbs and crushing her own spices and growing dodgy things in pots. Simon just eats it. He says you should never ask what it is.' She watched him sit on the window seat. 'In my last place all we had were takeaways, so it makes a change.'

They had come downstairs to make the tea because for a moment up there it had all been too much. Now, taking the mug and wriggling her knees up on the sofa, she realized that though telling the story was an immense ordeal for her, it was not for him. For Josh it was just someone else's life, with that slightly-unreal-not-really-my-problem feel to it. It would never matter as much to him. There would be minutes and hours, even today, when he would forget all about it.

He said, 'We ought to go out. It's easier to talk walking round. Play crazy golf. Feed the ducks.'

She nodded.

For a moment the warm silence of the house lay between them. Behind him, through the window, she saw the rhythmic perfection of the opposite facade.

She said, 'Caitlin always had a thing about birds. She would run round the playground with her arms out, pretending to be an eagle, or an aeroplane. I think she believed that if you flap your wings hard enough you can fly.'

'She couldn't have . . .'

'We were kids. Try to remember when you were a kid. It's all different . . . the way you think.' She sipped her tea and then put the mug down. It clicked on the glass table.

'The man came up towards us, and she was scared. She backed away, and she said, *If you come close, I'll jump*. It stopped him. He said, *Don't. I won't hurt you*. It was raining, and I was crying and everything was blurred and awful. And then there was this gust of wind. She . . . she sort of wobbled.'

'Why didn't you run?'

'Past him? That was the only way down.'

'But . . .'

'We couldn't run, Josh. We were frozen.' She had her

arms around herself; she knew she was rocking and held herself still. 'Caitlin had hold of me and she was too close to the edge and suddenly I knew that if she fell she'd take me with her. I was terrified. I yelled at her. But she had hold of my hand and she wouldn't let me go, she just wouldn't.' She couldn't keep still; she jumped up and started pacing through the room, to the door and back.

'Sulis, look . . .'

'NO. I need to finish. I was screaming and sobbing and I panicked and I tore myself away and then he was saying to her, *You can fly, little one. It's all right. It's safe.* And she turned. I saw his hand. It was on her back. She spread her arms. And then . . . Then she just went over the edge.'

Josh stared. 'He pushed her?'

'I saw her fall. Down and down. I saw her land.'

Someone laughed in the street. A car door slammed and the engine started. They listened to it drive away.

Finally he said, 'Did she . . . ?'

'She was dead.' Sulis sat. She felt totally calm now, in control. 'I turned round, but the man was gone. I probably fainted, because I don't remember anything else. I woke up all cold and stiff, huddled in the straw in the folly room – it was the next morning. I was all alone. I went down the steps and outside and she lay there all crumpled. I looked at her and then I knew it hadn't all been some nightmare. It was the last time I saw her, but

I'm glad I did because it wasn't horrible. She was so pale. Beautiful, like a broken china doll. There was hardly any blood. Then people were shouting and running towards me and it was all chaotic. The police took me away.'

'But he . . .'

She looked up. 'They never caught him, Josh. That's what this is all about. I'm the only one who knows what he looks like, and they never caught him.'

In the park, they walked against the wind. The tourist bus cruised slowly below the Royal Crescent, all the camera lenses on one side of the bus. She watched it warily. They paid for the golf clubs and spent a crazy hour knocking the ball through the small tunnels and twists of the course, its artificial turf luridly green against the red flags and the blue autumn sky. Then, kicking great drifts of fallen leaves, she told him about the investigation and the newspapers and the countrywide hunt for the killer.

'I was supposed to be protected but that one terrible photograph went around the world. That was when the threats started. A window was broken at our house. Stuff came through the post – I don't know, they never told me what. But we moved. And we just kept on moving.'

Coming to the lake, Josh stared out at the mallards and coots. 'Your mum?'

'She died a year later. Heart attack. She was only forty.'

Her voice was as bleak as the grey water. 'They said it had nothing to do with what happened, but I don't know . . . She was never the same after. Since then I've had about ten sets of foster-parents. And three times I've thought – maybe – I saw him. But nothing like this. He's really found me this time.' She turned, urgent. 'I know he has.'

'Then you should tell the police,' he said.

'NO!'

'Sulis . . .'

'Do you think I haven't tried that! It's useless. They just think . . . last time they made it totally clear they thought I was imagining things.' She flushed as she remembered the infuriating inspector who'd come to Alison's office, looking at his watch and making doodles instead of notes. 'They think I'm a hysterical schoolgirl. They don't think I'm in any danger. They don't get it. He's out there, and only I know what he looks like. Who he is.'

The mallards were crowding now, the males in their glossy winter colours. She took out the bread and seed, and threw a handful, watching how the bigger ducks snapped it up.

'That one.' Josh pointed.

A small coot dived for seed that showered him.

Sulis tossed out more, concentrating on sharing it evenly. She liked to see the urgency of the birds, their jabbing swift grabbing of food. Birds were uncomplicated. Free spirits. Feeding them was doing something good, with no mixed-up feelings. She felt happy for a second, as if telling the old story had freed her too, for a while.

Josh was quiet, as if he was trying to digest it all. They walked round the Crescent and then down into town, through the market to the art gallery, where they wandered aimlessly round an exhibition of plans and drawings.

One of them was by Jonathan Forrest. It looked like the plan of the Circus, so she stared at it a while, but it was complex, all lines and angles, and it made her restless, as if her eyes were led constantly by the movement of the shape.

'I should be getting back,' she said on the pavement.

Josh shuffled his feet in the gutter. 'Sulis, listen. We need to sort this. We need to find out if this man is really him.'

'You mean you don't believe me.'

He shook his head. 'It's not that. I asked Tom about the weirdo. Turns out he's just a local tramp. He's been here years – they all know him and he's harmless. He was here long before you came. So you see, it can't be him. And the man on the bus might have been anyone.'

She stared at him. He said, 'Don't be so scared.'

'I'm not scared.'

'You *are* scared. It seems to me you've been scared ever since that day. If you don't stop running, you'll be

157

looking over your shoulder all your life.' He jumped up out of the way of a car, and she saw how he got soaked from the spray and didn't even notice it.

She was too interested to be angry. 'Is that what you really think?'

He pulled her back into the entrance of the gallery. 'We'll make sure. We'll set a trap.'

'A what?'

'A trap. We'll catch him on camera. CCTV. I get a few hours in the office most days. I can set something up. Leave it to me.'

'At the baths?'

'Where else?'

The idea chilled her. All right, it terrified her. He was right about that. She stared at him through the sudden rain and the passing cars and the crowds of shoppers. 'NO,' she said.

'What?'

She turned and walked away, but he ran after her. 'Sulis! Why not?'

'I don't want to. And don't you dare, Josh! I mean that. Don't you dare set anything up without telling me.'

She was shaking and cold. The old dread had broken out all over her like sweat. She crossed the street and walked quickly over the bridge, not looking back to see if he was there or not. But he said, 'Running again, Sulis.'

She stopped.

Then deliberately she walked off the bridge into the

straight, perfect street called Great Pulkney Street, into its regular golden beauty, as if this was a place to breathe, as if the insistence on order would calm the hammering of her heart.

Josh didn't follow. He stood at the corner and said, 'I'll ring you tomorrow. Think about it. We could end all this, one way or the other.'

When she turned round, he was gone.

She walked home. Through the fleeting clouds the moon lit roofs and chimneys. A crowd came out of the matinee at the theatre, and enfolded her like a warm, chattering tide.

Simon was in the hall with the elderly woman from the lower flat.

'Thanks, Joan. I'll look after it.' Turning, he saw her. 'Oh so you're back. Want to see the cellars?'

'What?'

He held up a key. 'Jonathan Forrest's foundations? I thought I'd check the place out before the drain people get hold of it.'

She followed him back out on to the pavement, then down the steps into the area, the open court below street level which had once been the servants' entrance. The basement flat was empty, its owner in London most of the time. But Simon turned away from the house, to face the wall under the pavement. There were two small doors in it. Selecting a key, he opened one and they both peered in, curiously. A small dingy cubby-hole, smelling of coal. A few dark lumps glistened in one corner.

'Well it's clear what that was for.' He closed it and slipped the key in the lock of the other door. 'God, this is stiff.' Rain ran down his fingers. 'Should've brought an umbrella. Hold this, Su.'

It was a torch. She took it and watched him struggle with the lock but really she was listening, because in the street above someone was walking around the Circus. Soft, steady footsteps. Slow, as if they searched for a particular house.

'Ah. Got it.'

The key crunched round. The footsteps stopped. Someone was standing right above her, on the pavement outside the house. If she stepped back she would see him . . .

'Here we go.' Simon heaved the door open; it was warped, the wood grating on the stones. He stepped in, and held out his hand for the torch. 'Coming?'

If she just took the step back and looked up they would be face to face. The man would be standing there, in his dark coat, his face marked with those scars and pockmarks. Or might it be someone else . . . just a man with a dog, or Josh, following her home to make sure she was OK?

She gave Simon the torch and he clicked it on. They saw a large cellar room, the walls dull stone. It ran back into darkness.

'Fabulous. Let's take a look.' He stepped cautiously over the gritty floor.

Quickly, she followed.

The cellar was far larger than she had imagined. The roof had a plain vault and the room was cluttered, the back half of it piled with old mattresses, broken furniture, a dustbin full of junk. It smelt of dust and the sweetness of mould.

Simon groped for a light switch but when the bulb finally lit it was weak and left the corners in deep shadow.

'Well. They certainly built the place to stand for ever.' He ran his hand down the wall. 'Not even that much damp. Did I tell you, Su, that they had to level the site before they started? This was a sloping hill; still is, actually, apart from the Circus.'

She nodded. All she could think was that she was standing underneath the pavement, maybe even the road. That being underground was the opposite of being so high in the sky that you started to think you could fly.

Simon shoved a laden table aside with a grunt and examined the floor. 'This is where the trench will go. Pretty small, so there won't be much to see. Maybe your friend Josh will be a bit disappointed. Why isn't he studying, anyway? He seems bright enough.'

She had no idea. She realized she had been so concerned with telling Josh her own story that she still knew next to nothing about him. 'Perhaps it's money.'

161

'Well, money is around, if you know where to apply.'
Simon had reached the back wall. His voice came, oddly
doubled by the vault. 'Forrest used good materials.
Hundreds of spiders. Oh . . .'

He was silent so she said, 'What?'

'A door. Locked. Come and see.'

She edged in beside him. In the back wall of the cellar
was a door so old that its blackened wood panels were
warped and rotting. Simon tugged at it. 'As old as the
house, I'd say. I'd love to get this open.'

He tugged again. Beyond the door, something slid
and rattled.

'Leave it.' Sulis stepped back. For a fleeting moment
the door seemed threatening, a solid warning. 'Are we
under the street?'

'Further. Under the grass, I should think. The tree
roots probably break into some of the cellars.' He edged
back, dirt smudged on his face, and she saw his grin of
enthusiasm. 'Just think of it, Su, an underground circle of
rooms, all hidden. Forrest must have seen prints of the
Colosseum at Rome, where there are rooms under the
central space. He had this crazy idea about games in an
arena, you know, before the stuffed shirts on the town
council got to him.' He took out a handkerchief and
wiped his forehead. 'I'm filthy. Hannah will kill me.'

'No she won't.' Sulis flashed the torch around.

He laughed uneasily. 'No. No she won't. Stupid . . .'

'Are we finished?'

'Oh yes. I think so.' He turned off the light, and there was only the torchlight, a narrow beam of the twenty-first century. At once the room beyond it seemed to sink back into an older time; the walls glistened, the ceiling descended to a dark overhang.

Sulis flickered the torch over the walls. Then she stopped and focused it. 'Look at that.'

He came back. 'Well. That's wonderful.'

The initials were carved deeply, in the keystone over the locked doorway. Z S 1754. And around them, something rough and circular.

Simon reached up and fingered them. 'This must be Zachariah Stoke. Fantastic, and unrecorded, as far as I know. I'll take a photo of it, and then we'll definitely get this door open.'

'He must have been young then.'

'Still an apprentice. I think he designed a few good things himself later, though I'm not sure.'

She glanced up at the letters again, aslant in the torchlight, their shadows deep, then followed Simon cautiously up the steps, but the pavement was empty. There was no one in the Circus. The lit circle of bright windows reassured her, brought back the feeling she had first had here, of safety, of enclosure, of ordinary people sitting down to tea. But as she turned on the step to close the door she saw that the central grass was dark, and under the trees shadows moved, rustling, as if the streetlamps only made them restless.

Zac

I should have been travelling in Europe. Well, the University, first, of course – Oxford, like my father & his father before him. Reading Greats, or Law – it would hardly have mattered what, because Oxford is about more than learning. It's there I would have met the important men, the future politicos & churchmen, the givers of patronage, the friends that can make a young man's career in the world. Lords & noblemen with great houses & landed estates. After that, I would have gone abroad. The Grand Tour. Paris, Venice, Rome. At this very moment I would have been lounging in some gondola on the Grand Canal, or sipping champagne in the salon of a society beauty in the Latin Quarter. Instead, here I was, soaked & tired & hanging in terror on to a ladder that rose up before me twenty rickety feet into the air.

'Take it zlow, mazter. Nice & zlow.'

George Fisher was just below me. Did the fool think I was going to race up & fall to my death!

'Don't worry,' I said, my teeth gritted tight. 'I intend to.'

What makes it worse is that Forrest, twice my age, had climbed it easily. He was up there already, on the platform, speaking to the masons, though he coughed now & wheezed.

I hauled myself up. My arms were sore & my shoes slid on the damp wood. The rungs were ridiculously narrow.

Of course, Forrest's son is the one who's abroad. Jack. Studying Palladio's work in Italy. One day he will come home & be his father's right-hand man & what will happen to me then?

'Come on, Zac! What's keeping you?'

I hate him when he's growling at me but I hate him more when he's laughing. As I scrambled up breathless & stepped out on to the planks I wondered what inner demons drove him, because everything has been going wrong on this site & he knows it. And yet he was in a wild mood today, as if the joy of the rising building was in him. I confess I felt it too, even as I gripped the rail like a man on the gallows & looked down.

The site was a maelstrom. A clamour of chipping & a haze of stone dust. All the stone is hauled rough from the quarries & dressed here, on the spot, to fit where it is needed, so the din of mallets & hammers was almost unendurable. Every man had a stone & was cutting it or chipping it or sawing it & the dustfog they made gusted down over the city like a snow. Streets & doorsteps & roofs were golden with it. Men & donkeys & dogs choked on it. As if we made not only the round world of this building, but its weather too. Sometimes we even blotted out the sun.

'Zac. Look here.' He was watching the base of one of the pillars being lowered into place. 'Take note of how they do this. Methods haven't changed much since the Greeks.'

The stone was hung from a wooden crane hoisted by a windlass. It swung menacingly past our heads; the men tugged & dragged it into place, the gang leader shouting down orders in some slang so ancient the bath-builders must have used it.

Forrest turned. 'This section is speeding up now. Once all the column bases are done the design will start to be apparent.'

'It looks like chaos to me.'

'Then you must do as I do. Come up here at night in the moonlight, when the place is quiet. Then you almost see it growing, Zac. Rising out of the ground like trees of stone.'

He had some papers in his hand. Quite suddenly I wanted to tell him what I'd done.

'Master . . .'

'We must watch Harris. His men are working faster but their cutting is shoddy.'

'Yes. So I see. But, sir . . .'

166

A hod of stone barely missed my ear. Seeing me jump, he laughed & clapped a hand to my arm.

'A building site is full of danger, Zac. Perhaps we should get down.'

'I wanted to . . . I have to tell you . . .'

He turned to me, his eyes brown & bright. 'What?'

I swallowed. 'Things have been going wrong . . .'

'Not more than usual.'

'The ashlar blocks that went missing. Four guineas worth of stone.'

'There are always thefts, Zac.'

'But have you thought . . . ?' I gulped & cursed myself & stammered on. 'Have you never thought in these last weeks that someone might be trying to damage the project. Even drive you out of business?'

Why did I say it? I stared at him & he stared back. He said, 'Why should I think such a thing? It's true that I cannot afford losses. We're existing on loans & borrowings & Ralph's goodwill. It's true that he's our only backer with any real money. Master Greye has been spreading his brainless gossip round the town. But, Zac, when the building is clear they'll be queueing up to buy & speculate & invest in it. It will be the most fashionable thing in Aquae Sulis . . .'

'I know. I know. But if you cannot finish . . . if someone else . . .'

His eyebrows rose. 'By God, Zac, I would never sell! This is my monument. My tomb. I would never—'

'Your tomb!'

He laughed. Now it was he that looked uneasy. 'Did I say that? A foolish thing to say. Aubrey – have you read him, Zac? – Aubrey writes that the builders of the great circles designed the structures as their own tombs. Druids of great power, their gravegoods gold & amber & jet. But look, I have to see to those footings down there. Keep a watch for our guests, Zac!'

He was gone, swinging himself down carelessly. I watched him & it made me dizzy & I longed to sit down but there was nowhere. Men shoved past me. I was horribly in the way. Leaning on the rail, I closed my eyes. I had tried to tell him. And that was stupid because if I did I would be dismissed. And what had happened to my fierce anger & my pride? Where had they gone? Is everyone as changeable as this, or is it just me?

'Zac!'

My eyes opened.

Sylvia was below, with a parasol to keep off the dust. She waved. 'Come down. Show me around!'

For a moment I stared at her & then I swung myself down, awkward. A few of the men gave me a good-natured shove or hand; I reached the ground breathless & dishevelled but Sylvia was gazing round in delight.

'Look at it! It's wonderful. So many people all working on one thing . . . on Master Forrest's ideas.'

She was dressed in a pale blue silk outfit & looked well. Her complexion has quite cleared now, her red hair shines. She was pretty before but Forrest's care has restored her almost to beauty.

'Stop staring at me.'

'I'm not. I just . . .' I shrugged.

She spun the parasol. 'It's not like Master Peacock to be tongue-tied.' Then she stepped away & looked slightly flushed. 'Or is it that you're ashamed to be seen with me out of the house.'

'Of course not.' People were looking. I offered her my arm. 'Come on. I'll show you the site.'

We walked together along the half-finished section. The calm sweep of the facade amazed her. She gazed up at it & said quietly, 'He is a genius, isn't he.'

'Probably.'

'You're so lucky, Zac!'

'Am I?'

'To be able to work with him on this. To learn about design & architecture & history! I would give anything to be a boy & have those things.'

I stepped over a pile of bricks. 'It's hard work. And sometimes dull as dirtwater.'

She shrugged. 'One day women will study & build.'

'I very much doubt it. Women don't have the brains.'

She glared at me, & then when she saw I was teasing her she laughed. I laughed with her. Her arm was delicate in mine. For a moment I felt happy, & proud to show off the site, as if it was my own. 'Those are the stones . . . there . . . to be used for the first floors. These are the carpenters' lodges – I believe they're cutting the sash window frames. Over there you see Will the Smith hammering out hinges.'

'And you're in charge of it all.'

I was not, & yet for a second I hesitated to tell her so. But she laughed, arch as ever. And then she turned away, a little too quickly.

I glanced behind me. One of the workmen was leaning there, watching us. I could not be sure, but I felt I had seen him before, lounging outside Gibson's.

My sunny mood turned to acid. I said, 'Does all this really interest you, Sylvia, or are you just finding out all you can for Compton?'

My tongue is always my own worst enemy. She pulled away from me, a jerk of shock and anger.

'If that's what you think then goodbye, Zac. I can walk around on my own.'

I let her go for a moment, & ducked into the shelter, & stood there warming my hands, brooding.

The doorway behind me darkened.

I turned.

The workman I had recognized stood there. Close to, he was a thick-necked, poxy thug. He said, 'Message, zurr. From a gennleman we both know.'

I wouldn't be played with. 'Compton sent you? How dare—'

'Just to remind you of your debt, zurr. And to tell you not to speak to Forrest. You're too far in now.'

I stared at the rogue in disbelief.

'And as the mazter said, zurr, the site be dangerous. Stones slip from the scaffolding. Pitfalls and muck be everywhere. Anything might happen.'

For a moment then I felt a stab of fear such as I had never felt. I shoved past him & out into the dust & clatter, grabbing the arm of a mason. 'Have you seen a . . . lady? Young, in blue, with a parasol? Did you see where she went?'

He winked at me. 'I did zee. Couldn't miss she.'

'So where, man?'

He jerked his head. 'Them cellars. Zirr.'

I hurried over. The cellars were rooms built on the natural level of the site, but when everything was finished they would be underground, the earth piled & levelled above them. Now they were treacherous heaps of piled masonry. What was she doing there?

As I drew near I saw a closed carriage waiting, the windows up, the coachman smoking a pipe & glooming vacantly into space. Many idlers came to stare at the site, there were often carriages & sedan chairs about, but the dark anonymity of this one worried me. I ran into the first room, the raw stonework golden-yellow.

'Sylvia? Where are you?'

I heard her. She was talking, her voice low & urgent. I fumbled my way through the uneven mounds round to the next cellar, its roof open to the skies. Squeezing between a barrow & a wall, I edged closer.

Or to be honest, I crept. Because now I did not want her to hear me.

She said, 'I never wanted to see you again.'

'If that was true, you would have left the city.'

The voice was Compton's. I closed my hand into a fist against the cold brickwork.

'If I had had anywhere else to go . . .'

'You don't fool me, Sylvie. I hold you by an invisible thread, don't I? It's called your past.'

They were close to me; on the other side of the wall. But I had to strain to hear them over the racket of chipped stone & rumbling wheels. I stepped nearer.

He was laughing now. 'I have to say you're looking very well. Being Forrest's mistress suits you.'

'I'm not his mistress!'

'No? That's what all the town thinks.'

'It's what you tell them!'

I saw his shadow shrug easily. 'Not only me. There are plenty of gossips in Aquae Sulis. It's full of idle tongues & rich ladies with nothing else to do & a great love of scandal. Are you telling me you simply work for him?'

'He . . . I keep his house.'

He snorted, & Sylvia snapped, 'How can I explain Forrest to someone like you! He treats me like his daughter. Is kindness so rare?'

'Yes. No one does anything for nothing. Maybe he wants some strange druidical sacrifice for the foundations of his round temple. Be careful, Sylvie.

You & I know obsession is dangerous.'

I could see them now. He had his hand on her arm, was holding her close. She swore at him – a word I was amazed to hear from a girl – & she pulled away. He stepped after her, so I came at once around the wall & stood before him.

If he was surprised he covered it well.

'Master Zac. Always the gallant.'

'Let her go,' I said.

'I hardly think Sylvie needs you to defend her. I've seen her fight in the gutter & blacken the eye of at least two men.'

That rattled me, though I pretended it did not. 'I would rather you let her go.'

For a moment he was still. Then he took his hand from her arm very slowly. 'You know what she was, of course?'

'I don't—'

'Care? I doubt that. She was a girl who lured foolish rich young men into the gaming house. Even me, when I was innocent. She worked for the woman who runs the place. What other services she offered I can only imagine.'

She slapped him, a hard slap to the face with nothing ladylike about it. It would have floored me but Compton stood it, though he went as pale as milk & his anger was like ice in his voice.

'By God, Sylvie, I will destroy you for that.'

They glared at each other. I felt that I had stepped into an old quarrel; that they had known each other for much longer than I had guessed. I stood aside to let him pass. 'You will leave. Now.'

He drew himself up. For the first time I noticed his coat, with its black velvet collar. The silver walking stick that made my father's gift look like matchwood.

He didn't leave. He said, 'You've been doing what I asked?'

I could feel my teeth gritting. I glanced at Sylvia. 'What have you done?' she snapped.

Something choked me. Maybe it was shame. Maybe it was just anger that she was standing there, hearing this.

So I said, 'Not enough to persuade Forrest to give up. He will never give up the Circus. He has sworn it. So you had better forget your scheme.'

He shrugged, lazily. 'But you owe me a debt, Zac. A hundred guineas. Have you forgotten already?'

'You promised . . . If I did what you asked. And I have done it.'

'Did I?' The beauty spot was painted slightly larger today. 'But you see I am no further forward.'

'He'll never sell to you.'

'Then I'll have to change my scheme. I will build a rival Circus. And you will steal me a copy of his design.'

I stared. 'What?'

'You have two weeks. After that I call in the debt & you rot in a debtors' prison.'

I could have told him that I had altered the plans, that I had introduced subtle defects into the design, but as I stared at him I knew he would laugh at me. What was that to him? What did he know about the nuances of harmony? He wanted Forrest ruined, nothing else. I glanced at Sylvia. I needed time to think. Maybe I could use this change of plan.

'All right,' I said quietly. 'Whatever you want. But don't call in the loan. My mother . . . it would finish her.'

He took a breath & smiled. 'So nice to find a loyal son.'

Sylvia was watching me & I could hardly bear her eyes. But before she could say anything, other voices disturbed us, & to my horror Ralph Alleyn strolled around the wall & stood staring at us.

For a moment we were all frozen. Then he turned quickly, as if to head Forrest off, but it was too late. My master ushered a group of ladies & men around the masonry & we all saw each other in one startled instant.

These must be the guests. I had no idea who they were.

Compton recovered first. He bowed elegantly, & then we all did, as if a group of statues had awkwardly come to life.

Forrest's dark eyes fixed on him, then Sylvia. Then on me.

'Lord Compton.'

'Mister Forrest.'

Compton turned smoothly to the group. 'Ladies & gentlemen. Allow me to introduce Master Stoke, & Mistress . . . Sylvia.' He made a grimace, comically apologetic. 'I'm afraid I have never quite discovered her surname.'

I swear that even in the racket of the site I heard the silence that followed. It was as sharp as knives, & into it Compton bowed again & walked away. The women in the group were red-faced; one had her fan fluttering over her cheeks. Alleyn glared at me; I glanced away in hot embarrassment. Nothing had been said, but nothing needed to be said. Compton had made it quite clear what sort of girl Sylvia was, & these respectable, fat females were outraged even to be in her presence.

I couldn't even look at her. But Forrest did. He stepped out of the group & to my astonishment he took her hand & kissed it, very swiftly.

'Sylvia is my ward,' he said. 'I am going to adopt her.'

I stared at him; so did Alleyn. Syvia looked astonished, but she managed a smile & a pretty curtsey. Forrest turned to his guests, gently dropping her fingers. His brown coat was smudged with mud & his boots were filthy. The ribbon that held his hair back was loose. He looked more like one of the contractors than a genius & scholar. He gave me a look that said, 'Look after her,' & led the group aside. 'Now, allow me to show you the completed plans for the King's Circus. These will be houses everyone will long to buy . . .'

His voice faded as he ushered them towards the office.

Ralph Alleyn was left with Sylvia & myself. He said to me fiercely, 'Take her home. And you, girl, for God's sake stay out of sight. Do you want to ruin us all!'

She turned & I ran after her. We walked stiffly off the site & down the lane to the city. Halfway there she stopped dead, not looking back.

I knew she was crying.

Silent, I gave her my handkerchief. She grabbed it & turned aside into a little garden & sat on a seat there, mopping at her eyes, hands gripped into fists. 'I'll kill him.'

'Don't be foolish.'

'Rather than let him ruin Forrest I will.' She glared up at me. 'And you! With your yes sir, please sir! If you lie down he will ride over you, Zac.'

I looked away. Then I said, 'You realize those people were possible investors. They will have nothing to do with the project now. It was written all over them.'

'You needn't tell me.' Her voice was tense. 'And Forrest won't blame me, but it's my fault. I should go.'

'Did you know he would say that? About adopting you?'

She laughed, fierce. 'Of course not! He's a mystery to me. How can a man be so brilliant & difficult & bad-tempered & kind all at once? Is it the strain, do you think, of seeing into the future? Seeing what no one else can see, how the world will look if they let him build it? How can I let him adopt me! What will his son say!'

We were silent, looking down at the city. Then I swung my sword-stick. 'I may have sounded weak back there but I assure you, Sylvia, I am not. It was all a ruse. I want to take Compton down for myself. So I think I will concoct a plan.'

She looked up, her eyes blue & wet. 'A plan?'

'A most ingenious & careful plan,' I grinned. 'After all, isn't that what architects are trained to do?'

Bladud

I chose the circle.

Think about it. There is no other shape so pure. From its centre each point on the circumference is always the same distance away.

It is the shape of the sun. It encloses those within and rejects those without.

It is the oldest magic.

And yet in all nature there is nothing so rare as a perfect circle.

We raised stones. We found them far to the west, stones of healing, and a druid of power from that place transported them to the site for me, a man who lingers at the edges of legends, a man with the name of a bird.

When he left me his last words to me were, 'Spread your wings, O king.'

His advice intrigued me. But first we built. How we worked! Day after day in the heat and ice and rain we raised the stones, forming the circle that would stand for ever.

I was not content with a stark ring, not now. This was a
building, a temple and a healing place. So I capped the stones
with others, and had them carved with hidden, secret designs.
This was my clock. It would mark the years and the months
and the days, the turning of the sun.
There would never be another building like this.

Sulis

Josh's plan was simple.

On Wednesday Sulis had to work late. It was the night the Roman Baths Museum stayed open until nine; this was the first time she'd be working that shift. Somehow Josh had managed to get himself on the rota for the security room on the same night – Big Tom, apparently, was going to his daughter's party at the pub, so Josh would have the control room to himself . . . He'd told her this by text last night, as she'd watched a quiz show on TV with Simon shouting out all the answers and Hannah telling him to be quiet, angel, and the heavy old cat, Mousy, digging its claws into her knee.

But as Sulis rang up a sale on the till on Wednesday afternoon she wondered what use it all was. Surely *he* – the man who had no name, the man who haunted her like a shadow – would never dare to come inside here. Counting out the change she tried again to remember his face. In her dreams it was clear, but when she woke it was lost as if there was some blur there, some unresolved image. How would he know she was here late tonight? But of course, if he waited outside, he would see that she didn't leave at five.

She shivered. Handing over the change she glanced up at the clock and saw that it was already four thirty.

'Take your break, Su,' Ruth said. 'Now while it's quiet.'

The staffroom was a rather dingy grey office down a panelled corridor. Josh was the only one there, stirring a mug of tea and working on a newspaper crossword. He looked up. 'I thought you'd never get here!'

'We had a school group come through. They bought about ten million pencils and rubbers.' Flicking the kettle on she leaned against the table. 'Josh, this is never going to work. The shop . . .'

'You're not in the shop.'

'What?'

He filled in an answer and sat back, looking pleased with himself. 'For late nights there's a smaller staff – only about six of us – and the rota changes. Jen will be in the shop; they'll put you downstairs.'

'In the museum?'

He nodded. 'Walking about, keeping an eye on things.' He looked at her. 'It will be dark, and quiet. Not many people around. If he's coming in, he'll come tonight.'

They were silent. The kettle boiled, and she poured

out the hot water, feeling the heavy mug tremble in her hand. She sat by him. 'I don't know . . .'

'We talked about this.' He pushed the paper away and turned to her. 'You can't go on running away. You have to face him. See who he is . . . if it's him. You owe it to Caitlin.'

The name made her heart jump. 'What I don't understand is how. How did he find me here? We were so careful – new name, new parents, everything. It doesn't make sense.'

Josh was silent a moment. Then he said, 'We don't know it's him. The man in the street – the one on the bus – they might just have been different people. Ordinary people. Are you really sure they were the same?'

She glared at him. 'Yes.'

'If it is him, he must be trying to scare you. The police . . .'

'Not till I'm sure. I want to be sure, Josh.' She sipped the tea. She was shivering and it wasn't from cold. 'What do I do?'

'Just make sure you stay in the lit places where the cameras are. I'll follow you from the control room. I'll be watching you all the time and as soon as you spot him just give me the nod and I'll get him on film.'

'And if he spots me first?'

'I'll hit every alarm we have. And that's quite a few. But he won't. He won't know we're ready for him.' He looked at her. 'Will you be able to do it?'

She had no idea. But he was right. She wanted an end to this. To the long succession of different houses and ever-changing people. She wanted a place that would be home. A city that would be perfect.

'I can do it.'

He was watching her and she didn't know what he was thinking. So she said, 'I forgot to tell you. Simon and I went into the cellars under the Circus last night – there's a blocked-up door down there that he's really interested in. He says come tomorrow and help him open it.'

'Great.'

Neither of them mentioned that her whole world might be shattered by tomorrow. To keep the moment safe she said, 'He asked me about you and I couldn't really answer. Why aren't you at uni?'

Josh looked surprised, then annoyed. He had a distant, acid look sometimes, as if he felt he was better than anyone else – it came on his face now. 'Maybe I don't want to be.'

'Maybe I'm not that stupid.'

He shrugged. 'Then don't ask.'

'Why not? I told you my story – it can't be anywhere near as bad as that.'

'It's not. I did the first year but then I dropped out, right? My father's business went bust – he left, my mother needs the money. That's it, that's all. No big deal. I'll get back there. I don't intend to spend the rest of my life in a dead-end job like this.'

'Fine. Now I know.'

'Now you know.'

He was silent, relentlessly filling letters into the grid. She wanted to shake him. Did he have no idea how scared she was, that she had only asked so that she could think about something else?

He wrote the last word in and stood up, and it was only when he turned at the door that she saw how upset he was, under that haughty way he had. He said, 'Remember. Stay by the cameras. Especially near the sacred spring, because of the steam.' Then he was gone.

The door slowly closed on its hinge.

She sipped the scalding tea, barely noticing how it burned her tongue.

The underground part of the museum was oddly warm, as if the layers of earth above insulated it. She walked around quietly, glad there were people here. A tourist asked if he could take photos, and then two American women asked her about the gorgon mask, its fierce mustachioed face looking down as they discussed it.

'It would have been on the pediment of the temple,' she explained.

'I see. And where was the temple, exactly?'

She led them through the rooms to the wide flat stone steps that led up only into a blank wall.

'Here. This was the entrance. But the temple itself – if it still exists – is under the buildings around the square

– the cafe opposite and the shops and under Stall Street. I don't think it's ever been excavated.'

'You mean it's still down there? Amazing!'

When they were gone she stayed a moment, standing on the Roman steps, imagining how people in togas would have been brushing past her, going in and out, ancient distant people with different gods and different speech. How what was now underground had once stood in the sunlight.

She turned round and caught the gaze of the gorgon face.

It frowned down at her.

Was this Sulis? Was Sulis male or female? Everyone said a goddess but this face was male. Maybe it was Bladud, because under it was one of the artist's weird pigs, this one made of wood, polished as shiny as a seed. She shook her head. Art, like archaeology, was baffling. It only ever showed fragments.

The word made her think of Josh and she glanced up at the camera, realizing he would be watching her through it. She made a face at it. The camera moved and clicked slightly on its bracket.

An hour later she was bored and tired. She had patrolled the museum and there was no one in it. The whole place was empty.

What was the use of a late night if no one came?

She leaned against the glass case of pewter curses. These were her favourite things down here – they fascinated her, these ancient messages and prayers once scratched on soft metal and thrown in the water to the spirit of the spring. They were in Latin, but the translations were typed out next to them.

To the Goddess Sulis Minerva . . . I give to your divinity the money which I have lost and may he who has stolen it be forced to . . .

. . . A curse on the one, whether pagan or Christian, man or woman, boy or girl, slave or free, who has stolen from me, Annianus, in the morning, six silver pieces from my purse . . .

There must have been a lot of thieving in those old times. Some things didn't change. She liked the ones that were more bloodthirsty.

. . . These are the names of those who have sworn at the spring to the Goddess Sulis on the twelfth of April . . . Whosoever has lied you are to make him pay for it to the Goddess Sulis in his own blood . . .

That one gave her an idea. She felt silly, but she pulled out a pen and a scrap of paper and wrote her own message on it.

To the Goddess Sulis Minerva. There is someone following

me. He killed Caitlin. I want you to punish him for what he did. I want you to end the shadow on my life . . .

Stupid.

But she scrumpled it up and walked through the museum to the sacred spring where the bubbling water steamed gently. Then she saw the camera tracking her. She didn't want Josh seeing this.

So she went round to the outfall, the dim narrow corridor where the water rushed in a great steaming hiss down and through a drain to the great bath outside. The lip of the stone was mustard yellow with the iron of the water, smooth as wet marble.

She threw the tiny ball of paper in and the water took it instantly, whisking it away under its surface, sluicing it down into the dark. As soon as it was gone she felt a terrible dread. She had a silly desire to get it back, because she had cursed him now, and what might that mean?

She breathed out. Over the steaming roar of the water she made herself smile. There was no goddess in the spring. That was all a long time ago, and the world had changed. But she took out a five-pence piece, and threw it in as an offering, not because she believed, but because there were other coins in there, glinting sloping circles deep under the surface.

Movement.

She caught it in the water, a flash of reflection.

Someone was standing behind her.

She didn't turn. She couldn't move. But she knew he was there, at her back, dark as her shadow, tall and dark in the steamy warmth of the spring.

He said, *Sulis.*

Or was it the whirr of the air-conditioning, the hiss of the water?

'Who are you?' Her whisper was lost in the steam.

You know who I am. You have to release me, Sulis. You have to let me fly like a bird.

Fragments of a face. An eye, a cheekbone, a frowning forehead fractured in the churning water. Was she seeing him, or herself, or the gorgon mask up on the wall behind them both?

And where was Josh?

She said, 'You killed her.'

My hand. On her back.

'You pushed her.'

I had to get her away from me.

'You murdered her.'

I released her.

Where was Josh? She turned, but the man was walking away from her into the gloom of the room. She said, 'Wait. I don't know . . . if it's you.'

He didn't stop. He just said, *Follow me, Sulis* and the steam opened and he was gone. She yelled, 'JOSH!' and ran, into the room where the steps of the temple rose into the unexcavated wall, and she was sure for a moment she saw him there, climbing the steps that led nowhere. But the wall was blank. And then she was racing around the displays, the altars, the models of the baths, straight round a partition into Josh, whose hand grabbed her and whose breathless voice gasped, 'Where? Where is he?'

'He was there. Back there!'

'He can't have got out. I've locked the door.'

She stared at him, appalled, but this was a new Josh. He had a big handtorch and he turned the lights up to their maximum. 'Right.' His voice was calm and he gave her a glance that puzzled her. Then he called out, 'HELLO! If there's anyone in here, can you come out now please! The museum is closing.'

Heads of Roman gods and faces on stone gazed at him impassively. Nothing moved in the dim rooms.

'He's got past us,' Sulis said quickly.

'No chance.'

'But . . .'

'Come on, Sulis, let's look.' He kept his eyes on hers, challenging. 'You're not afraid to look, are you?'

'No, but if . . .'

Josh took her hand. He led her quietly around the suite of underground spaces, and though it was dark and shadowy he flashed the torch everywhere and explored every inch, even the steamy depths of the 'fall and the spring. By the end he was almost 'ng her; she snatched her hand away and stood, fuming, understanding.

'You don't believe me, do you! You don't think he was ever here!'

He turned, his shadow against the wall. 'He wasn't. The place was empty. I had everything on camera.'

'No you didn't. I was at the outfall. There isn't a camera that can see in there.'

'All right. I could only get part of that. But, Sulis, I could see everywhere else. The entrance hall, the other rooms, the baths. There was no one at all in here but you.'

For a moment she just stared at him. Then she turned and ran, out through the empty rooms, up the steps to the open-air bath, its magical waters fogging the frosty night.

Around it the colonnade was dark, the figures of Roman emperors gazing down at her. She heard Josh come out behind her.

'Look . . . don't get upset . . .'

'I'm not upset.' She was shaking. She ran down the cracked paving, through the door the public didn't use, down a corridor and into the marble splendour of the entrance hall.

A woman called Martha was on reception, closing up.

Sulis said, breathless, 'Did a man come in tonight . . . late? Last in, even?'

Caught halfway through counting coins, the woman

looked up, preoccupied. 'Sorry no . . . well, what did he look like?'

Sulis frowned. She knew Josh was behind her, waiting for the answer. She heard the torch click off in his hand.

'Tall. Dark.' It sounded so useless. 'Thin. Sort of . . . pockmarked face.'

Martha poured the coins into the bag. She tapped the calculator off. 'No, no one like that. The last people in were an elderly couple and their grandsons and that was about an hour ago. They'd have left by now. No tall dark handsome strangers all night, Sulis. I'd have noticed!'

Sulis turned. Pushing past Josh she marched straight to the door marked SECURITY and once inside she stared at the baffling bank of screens. Each was lit with a shadowy corner of the museum.

He came in behind her. 'I'll show you,' he said.

It took about half an hour. He ran everything at double, triple speed. She saw visitors blur like ghosts in the frames of time, there, not there, caught in strange, jagged motion. She saw the rooms empty, the shadows gather, the clock numbers jerk. She saw herself, gazing into cases, sitting on a chair, at one corner, at another doorway, talking, alone. She saw all this, but she didn't see the man.

Finally the last camera.

'This is what I was watching you on at the outfall.'

Josh kept his gaze deliberately away from hers. 'It's an awkward angle. But you can see for yourself . . .'

A shadowy shape stood before the archway of roaring water. It leaned out and tossed a small object through the grille. Her hand was clear, a pale glimmer that slowed as Josh slowed the playback. She saw her sleeve, one side of her face.

She saw herself turn, and speak. She had said, 'Who are you?'

But the camera showed only darkness, unresolvable mystery.

'Hold it there!'

He pressed pause. Together they stared at the grainy image, Sulis crouching so close to the screen her breath fogged it.

'There.' Her fingers touched the glass. 'There. Isn't that something? The sleeve of his coat? Right at the edge?'

She looked up. Josh was sitting on the table with the remote loose in his hands. He said quietly, 'Let's face it, Sulis. He wasn't there. No one was there.' He gazed at her hard. 'I don't know if it's me you're fooling, or just yourself. But I'll tell you what I think now. I think there hasn't been anyone there all along.'

The Circle

Can anything be a more glorious Image of the Sun than a circular wall, upon the summit of a hill, gilded with Gold?

Zac

Supper that night was a sadly quiet affair.

Forrest sat at the head of the table & ate rapidly. He never seemed to much notice what he ate; Mrs Hall could have served raw capon & carrots with the dirt still on & he would have swallowed them & wondered why he was sick afterwards. Sylvia picked at her food, watching me through the candlesticks. I tried not to look at her.

'Wine, Zac?' Forrest held out the bottle.

I lifted my glass & let him splash some in. Then I said, 'Those people, sir. At the site . . .'

He shrugged. 'Timid fools without vision. What can you do? We'll get no money from them.'

Silence again. He knew, & we knew, that their reluctance was widespread.

Suddenly he crashed down his knife & spoon & leapt up, pacing the room fiercely. 'Sometimes I think I am all alone in the world, do you know that? That I am the only man of this wretched city who can see what its future might be! Look at it! Overrun with beggars & dogs! A hovel in the hills huddling down, when it might be wide & stately & full of light.' He flung the curtains open, revealing the gaslit glimmers of the street outside, the smoky fog that wreathed the gracious square. 'What a place it was once. Full of power, full of magic! And it could be again. Wide clean streets, fresh air, high generous rooms, running water. What we could not do against poverty! Against disease!'

'You truly believe there was a great temple here?' Sylvia asked quietly.

'Yes I do!' He turned, his face alight. 'Since men first found the waters, this would have been a holy place. I believe there were two temples, Sylvia, one to the sun, & one to the moon. Ancient structures. They must lie under the lower part of the town, very near the baths.' He glanced back through the window. 'When I was working on the Mineral Hospital we found many things in the ground that proved there had been buildings there. Broken brick, carved stone. We found strange twisted pewter fragments. Even tiles.' He came back to the table & sat, leaning towards her. 'I wanted to design a circular building on that site, but the landowner objected. I seem to have spent all my life trying to create this thing. But at least now it will be built, even if I am ruined for it.'

'You will not be ruined.' She handed him his wineglass.

For a moment he looked at her, then at me. 'No,' he

said. 'I trust I will not be. Because the future needs me.'

He sipped the wine & some of the warmth faded from him. The light went out of his eyes. If all the world disappointed him, I thought, what must he think of me?

I said, 'Sir, may I ask you something?'

He said, 'Ask away, Zac.'

'It's just . . . the plan of the Circus. You said the central area is to be paved?'

'Yes, & . . .'

'So there is to be nothing there . . . even under the ground?'

He looked at me & his eyes were steady & dark as flint. 'Nothing, Zac. Nothing of importance.'

He lied. He gave me the lie to my face. In that instant I cared nothing for his designs, for his grand building. All I knew was that he truly did not trust me, he thought me a spoiled brat & a shallow wastrel & the knowledge went in like an arrow.

But I managed a smile.

While he & Sylvia helped clear the table I went out & sat on a bench in the garden. The stars were rising over the downs & Aquae Sulis was indeed no more than a foggy huddle in a fold of land, almost as if the ancient city still lingered there in the mist. I folded my arms against the cold & leaned back, my breath clotted with damp.

There was to be something secret at the circle's heart. Something to do with the Oroboros group he frequented. If he would not tell me about it I would ferret it out for myself. Because I would save him, & myself, & Sylvia, even if neither of them deserved me. I smiled coolly. Despite themselves, they would be in debt to me.

Her voice said, 'All puffed up again, Master Peacock.'

She crept on me so quietly! I jumped up, annoyed. 'Must you do that!'

She was not smiling. She perched on the bench next to me, her feet off the ground for the mud.

'Sorry, Zac. But sometimes you look so full of yourself, your secrets, your plans. All closed up inside, & proud.'

'I am not proud. I am nothing in this town, Sylvia. But I will not be stamped on by Compton.'

'So you have invented a plan?'

'I have already begun it.' This was, I have to confess, the part I had dreaded. But I took a deep breath & told her what I had done. 'This afternoon I sent a letter to Compton. It was badly written & spelled – I took great trouble with it. It was from you.'

She leapt up, mud or not. 'No!'

'Yes. I signed it *Sylvia*.'

'You had no right! I can't believe you had the gall . . .'

I stood too. 'You said you'd do anything for Forrest. I wish I knew if that was true.'

She glared. Her fury turned me cold. There was a small summerhouse at the bottom of the garden; a pleasant place in the summer but damp now & tangled with dead creeper. I grasped her arm & led her there, because I was afraid Forrest would hear us from the house.

200

Once inside she turned on me. 'Tell me what you wrote.'

I drew myself upright. I would not be hangdog before her, even though I felt guilty. 'I . . . you, that is . . . have told Lord Compton that I have done as he asked. He must meet you at the baths tomorrow night at eight. You will be bringing him the plans of the Circus . . .'

She gasped but I went on unflinching. 'In return he must hand over the note-of-promise I wrote him for the hundred guineas. I will be there, watching. In fact I will go with you. But I'll make sure he does not see me.'

'See your shame, you mean!' She pulled away from me & stood among the brambles. 'How can you do this, Zac! To your master! Can you hate him that much!'

'I don't hate him.' I did not want to talk about Forrest. 'I do this for myself. And let me set your mind at rest, Sylvia, since you obviously think the worst of me. The design I'm selling will not be Forrest's Circus. This will be a forgery, & it will be unbuildable.'

She stared.

Quietly, I explained about the copy I had made in my anger – the subtle alterations, the defects. She listened to all of it, her hand tugging dead leaves from the vine-covered pillar of the gazebo.

When I had finished she remained silent, gazing at me a long time. I shivered with the damp. My own sweat was cold on me.

'Why did you do it?' she whispered.

'That doesn't matter. It was a wild idea. Sometimes . . . sometimes I think all the world is against me. Perhaps I did it because I wanted to bring Forrest down, to introduce a flaw into his heaven. To be Lucifer to his God. I don't know. But, Sylvia, listen, you MUST get the note from Compton. Make sure it's the one I wrote – that it has my signature on. Otherwise I'll be ruined.'

'But when he finds out.' She was looking towards the house.

'He can't do anything without the IOU. I won't owe him a penny piece.'

'Not Compton, you fool!' Her face was pale. 'Forrest.'

I shrugged. 'If he has any sense he'll thank me. Because by then the Circus will be built & the houses sold & what will Compton have after all? Flawed designs for a project someone else has perfected. No, Forrest won't blame me for that.'

In the silent garden only the leaves dripped. A fine rain must be drizzling, because the lamp in the window of the house was fuzzy & mazy. I shivered. 'You will do it, Sylvia? Please say you will. It's my only chance.'

She pulled her shawl tight. For a moment I thought she would refuse; then she turned & unpicked her skirt from the thorns. When she looked up her face had that pert, sharp look that for the last few weeks had been fading. Now it was back.

She turned away from my scrutiny.

'Of course I'll do it,' she said.

* * *

All that day at the site I was oddly nervous. I made mistakes, lost things, daydreamed in the tiny stuffy office. Outside, the cacaphony of building went on around me; the facade of the first arc of the circle was in place almost to the second floors, but the doorways were stark empty rectangles & jackdaws flew in & out of where the windows would be.

I don't know if Forrest suspected me of prying, but there was no sign of the plans. He must have them locked up in the safe at home. Only the working sheets were here, the day's instructions to the masons. And underneath, his sketch book.

I sat & opened its battered leather cover.

The metopes.

Here they were, all the mysterious symbols & pictures that would be carved in stone to ring the finished building. What secret did they hold? A telescope. Two hands sharing a ring. A tree with what might be a standing stone behind it. Did they tell a story? Did they mean anything? Was this my master's message to the future, or his joke against it?

I looked again at the metope of the two hands. He had drawn them ringed with what might be cloud, or flowers. Were they a pair? Or were the hands of two different people, meeting here opposite each other, each grasping half of the circle? His hand & mine? Mine & Sylvia's?

I turned the pages, puzzling them out. The oak tree,

snakes round a spade, a mirror, a sickle. At one corner a horse's skull hung with flowers or maybe bells. The whole mystery of his mind was here. A secret, that if I might decipher it would . . .

'Mazter? We need ee.'

The workman glanced curiously at the book. I shut it with a snap. 'What?'

'Tiz at the chamber.'

'What chamber?' I swivelled in my chair & let my irritation show. 'What are you talking about, man?'

These men never even notice annoyance. He said, 'The covert room Mazter Vorrest wanted.' He looked at me with a sly nod. 'You know the one.'

I had no idea. I said slowly, 'Ah. Yes. That one.'

'She beyond the zellars. The one he has my gang on, working secret.'

I sat up. 'Of course. What about it?'

'Something odd there, zirr. In the foundations. Only, the mazter has gone up to the quarry, so . . .'

I jumped up. My heart was racing. 'Show me.'

The foreman's name was Fisher. I had often seen Forrest talking to him. A trusted man, evidently. He led me through the site & into the half-finished cellars. I hurried after him, stumbling, trying to keep my boots from the muck, & trying to look as if I knew exactly where we were going. But my mind was racing ahead of me. Was this what Forrest was keeping from me? *The chamber?*

I climbed over uncut stone. Wooden cranes swung blocks of ashlar over my head.

He led me into the one cellar that had been roofed. The floor was trampled dust, & the stone vaults fresh & gold. At the far end was a great heap of wood, scaffolding planks perhaps, piled high to the roof, out of the weather.

I stopped but he glanced back through the dimness. 'Beyond, zirr. These are to hide the work.'

I hoped I had not shown him my ignorance. I nodded, loftily, & pushed past him. Behind the wood in the brick wall was an archway, half built, the keystones lying on the floor like pieces of a child's puzzle ready to assemble.

Beyond the arch was a passageway. We walked down it, into the chamber.

'There's some water coming up.' Fisher gestured to where a spade lay on the ground. I walked across, the rubble & brick fragments crunching under my boots. A circular chamber – well that was to be expected. The roof was domed, like a beehive. Golden stone walls curved down to the bare floor. In the apex of the dome was darkness, but I felt a draught. An airshaft, somewhere.

The man watched me as I walked across to the centre. My heart thudded so loudly I was sure he would hear it. This was the very centre of the Circus.

But what was it for?

'Do you zee?' He pointed.

'I see.'

Water was oozing from the floor. It had collected in a small puddle. I glanced up. 'Are you sure it's not dripping in from the roof?'

He laughed, a short gruff sound. 'It be hot, zurr.'

I reached out & dipped a finger in. Warmth. Small bubbles rose to caress my skin. I caught a faint steam in the air. 'Another spring?'

'I don't zee how. So far above the valley.'

I had no idea if that mattered. Certainly the other hot springs were below. I straightened up, wondering if Forrest had known by some alchemy that this would be here? But surely he had only chosen the site for the Circus because it was high, & the landowner was willing?

'What shall we do, mazter? Only Mazter Vorrest said naught about this & we have to finish today.'

I nodded. 'His instructions were?'

'Clear the room & lock it up.' His craggy face went crafty. 'For tomorrow night.'

I glared at him. 'What do you know of that? Master Forrest does not want his private business gossiped in the city.'

'Nor will it be. I only know They will be here tomorrow, & now there's this water.'

They must be the Oroboros. I was burning to know more, but had to appear as if I already did. So I said, 'Yes. Well, I suggest you get the men in & build a small reservoir there to hold the seepage. It does not seem to be a great flow. A small circular pool in the centre will not spoil Master Forrest's . . . ceremony.'

He gazed at me. For a moment we were both silent in the darkness. Then he said, 'Leave it to me, zirr.'

I turned & went out, trying to see as much of the room as I could in one glance. But it told me nothing. In the cellar I stopped. 'One more thing, Fisher. I will not tell the master you brought me here. He might be annoyed with you for it. Tell him, if he asks, that the pool was your own idea.'

The foreman grinned at me. He was not a fool, & I was sure he suspected me by now. But he touched his forehead and said only, 'Zirr.'

I could not keep still. I took my hat & stick & walked down the hill & rapidly around the alleyways of the city, thinking, planning. I went into a coffee shop in Quiet Street & ordered chocolate & stirred it until it was cold, thinking of what I would do. I would watch until Forrest left the house. I would follow him to the site & hide behind the pile of wood. I would see the mysteries of the Oroboros.

And perhaps I would understand, after all, the purpose of his circle of stone.

Bladud

What exists beyond perfection? Where is there to go after that?

I had built my city and it enclosed me. Stone and sky became my obsession.

And the words I had heard deep in the stillness of my mind began to echo there as if they could not escape. 'Open your wings, O king.'

Did I hear them or imagine them? I began to ponder, and I began to experiment.

I tried various woods to find the lightest and most pliable. I crafted them into wings, and then I climbed on to the high downs and called on the birds to offer me their help. By sorcery I brought them to my hands, the eagle, the sparrow, the crow, the kingfisher. Each gave me the ransom of a feather. I bound these in bunches, fixed them with pitch and resin. I sewed them with needles of bone.

I had been king for twenty years and there was no more work for me to do here. But the sky is limitless, and I would launch myself into it and I would fly.

Of all men, I would be the first to soar into whatever lies beyond.

No one believed in me. They called me a fool and deluded. They mocked my work. And sometimes, as I lay on my bed in the darkest nights, without the stars or the moon, I felt the cold of dread on me, and knew that I was mad.

One day I went to the hot pool and looked down into its depths and her face looked up at me. And she said, 'There's no way down from here, lord king. Unless you fly.'

Sulis

The room was dark. She liked it like that.

Hannah knocked on the door again. For the fourth time. 'Are you sure you don't want any breakfast?'

'Sure.'

'You have to eat something, Sulis.'

She didn't answer.

'I wish you'd talk to me.' The voice was close to the door. 'I can easily stay if . . .'

'No. I'm fine. You go.'

Hesitation. She could feel it through the white-painted panels. Whispers on a telephone. Then, after a while, footsteps, and the front door far below opening and closing.

Sulis lay with the bedclothes over her head. It was dark in here and warm, and there was no one to annoy her. She listened to the quiet of the house, the small hums of the fridge, the click of the heating. Pigeons cooed outside the window. An ice-cream van, somewhere a long way off, chundled out a merry tune . . . It reminded her of being very small, being off school with a cold or something. When Mum would bring things up on a tray and say, 'How are you feeling?'

The thought made her twist over and pull the sheets off her face. She took a deep breath.

The ceiling above was white. Reflected shimmers from cars in the Circus passed slowly round.

Josh's scorn came back to her again, but it had weakened in the days since he'd said it. *I think there hasn't been anyone there all along.*

Was he right?

At first she had been furious with him and raw with anger, but over the last days she couldn't help wondering, going over it all in her mind – the man on the bench, the man at the cafe table, the man in the bus. Each of them a dim, vague shape, a dark coat, a newspaper.

But the last one, in the museum. Surely she had seen him there.

Surely she had spoken to him.

She swung her feet out of bed, threw on a dressing-gown and went out. In the living room Simon's books were scattered. She glanced at them idly, then went to the kitchen and tipped some cereal into a bowl. The only milk was Hannah's soy stuff, and she hated it, but she poured it in and rummaged for a spoon.

Then she sat on the sofa.

Hannah had left in a hurry, because papers and make-up from her bag were everywhere, as if she'd lost her keys and been racing to find them. They were the scattiest couple Sulis had ever stayed with.

Eating the cereal, she saw the corner of the envelope first. It was lying upside down on the floor, half under the sofa. She slid it out with her foot, and worked out the address as she ate. And the name.

Mrs Alison West.

Sheffield Social Services.

Deliberately, she made herself finish all the cereal and even lick the spoon before she put the bowl aside and bent down and picked the envelope up.

For a moment she held it. Then she took it up to her room, opened the window, so that the cool morning air gusted in, sat on the bed and slid her finger under the gummed edge.

The paper tore.

Inside was a letter. And a form.

CONFIDENTIAL. Evaluation and Psychological Profile.

Please fill in any sections you feel to be relevant. All information is strictly in confidence. Subject . . . And then her name.

She pressed her lips together. Of course she had known they had to fill in things like this. Some of her foster-parents had shown them to her, moaning about paperwork. This one was pretty much like the others . . . her behaviour, her interests, her social skills . . . all boxes to tick. Did she have nightmares? Did she have friends?

But the letter was new, and as she opened it and read it her fingers shook and her vague feeling of guilt vanished in anger.

Hannah's scrawl was as gushing and rushed as its writer.

Dear Alison,

Just to report progress on . . . you know . . . the problems we discussed last night on the phone. I don't know what happened but I think now that the boyfriend . . . Josh . . . may have found out about Su's background. She's been very strange with us. Even more moody than usual. Not answering questions. In the evening she gets up and goes to the windows, maybe seven or eight times, and looks out into the street. All the things you told us to watch out for. She has absolutely no idea she's doing it, but she's said things that make it quite clear she's told Josh about Sheffield, and I think that may be the reason for his rejection of her. Certainly they've split up, and she hasn't been to work, and barely eaten, for the last three days. To be honest, I'm a bit out of my depth.

Sulis stared at the paper in disbelief.

What things had she said? She was never moody! A sudden terror washed over her, as if she no longer knew herself. As if the Sulis she was and the Sulis they saw were totally different people.

A tap at the window. She stared up, her heart

thudding, but it was only a jackdaw, hopping on the open sill. She waved at it, and it flew away, leaving one tiny feather that lifted in the wind.

It's a pity about the job, because I was beginning to feel it was helping her. I'm not sure if they'll hold it open for her . . . I've told them she's got flu. In fact it's more like a sort of nervous collapse. She barely gets out of bed. We're really concerned. I mean, I know when I was a teenager, the boy thing . . . well!!!! But with S's history it's so tricky. Another thing is that when she first came here she loved the city, but she seems increasingly unwilling to go out. It's a bit like the other times you spoke of – when she claimed to see the assailant. And yet we're certain no one knows who she is.

Sulis put the letter down. She didn't want to read any more. Claimed to see the assailant. Did that mean they – social workers, police – had never believed her either? Did it mean they were always watching her and analysing her and ticking little boxes about her and that they'd really never believed a word she'd said?

She went to the window and looked out.

When had it all started to go wrong, her perfect city? When had the flaws begun to show, the cracks in the facade? As if there were hidden errors, barely visible. Wrong proportions. As if the world was not quite upright.

She turned back and grabbed the letter and read the rest of it quickly.

. . . I really feel for her. Because it's all inside her and she won't let it out. We've decided we need to go and have a word with this boy, but to be honest I'm going to leave most of it to Simon. He's so much better at this sort of thing. Phone me, Alison, and we can talk. On my mobile, as usual.
Best wishes always,
Hannah.
PS The psychiatrist was right about the architecture thing.

She folded it and held it in her lap. She felt that everything that had been safe underneath her had suddenly collapsed. Simon talking to Josh? Behind her back? And what architecture thing, because Aquae Sulis had been her choice and no one else's. Or did she give herself away so easily?

She took the letter to the window, tore it into a hundred tiny bits and scattered them to the wind. Then she dressed, made her bed, grabbed her bag and went out. Afraid, was she? Let's see how afraid they would be to come back and find her gone.

She walked round the Circus, then browsed the shops and strolled round the Royal Crescent. Stubbornly, she stopped herself looking behind. Tourists were everywhere; people were photographing the sweeping arch of the crescent, its moon-shape crowning the hilltop. She bought some sandwiches and lay on her stomach in the warm grass of the park and gazed up at it.

Forrest had begun his dream, a sun temple, and someone else – his son, or his pupil – had finished it. The sun and the moon, in stone. Dreams laid out on the landscape, dreams become solid, to make people live and move in ways the architect had never imagined.

Suddenly she knew that one day she would do this. She would design buildings. The thought filled her with delight; she rolled over and laughed up at the blue sky.

Why had she never known that before? Because the knowledge had been there all the time, waiting. It had always been inside her, since the red and blue building-block towers she and Caitlin had raised on the board on the floor in the classroom.

The pleasure of it, of dreaming what her future would be, was like a warm unsealing inside her. She lay in the sun all afternoon, ignoring the tourists and the birds and some kids playing football until the sky began to darken and she realized she was stiff and hungry.

Rolling over she looked round.

The wide lawns were almost bare. No one sat near her. No one watched her. She was alone.

She picked up her bag, rummaged, and found her

mobile phone. There was one message – from Hannah.
Su. Where are you?

It must be about six. The sky was draining its light away into the west; a blue flecked with orange. She shivered, slightly chilled, and the elation of the afternoon went out like a doused candle, like a piece of music in her head stopping in mid-bar.

She went home.

As she came into the Circus she saw that someone was sitting on the bench on the grass, leaning over the back, watching her door. She stopped, stunned with fear. A dark coat. The shadowy figure half lost in the darkening street and the overhanging trees.

She went to turn away, then stopped. Where was there to go? And she wasn't going to bear this any longer.

She walked firmly round the circling street towards him.

As she got nearer, he noticed her. He turned his head, and stood up.

Her heart thudded. She walked right up to him and they looked at each other a moment.

Then Josh said, 'I was waiting for you.'

She was breathless. She managed to nod. 'Have they talked to you?'

'Who?'

'Hannah. Simon.'

'No.'

He was looking down at the grass. But she believed him, because he raised his head and said, 'Look, Sulis, about the other night . . .'

'Leave it. Forget it. We'll talk about it later.' She shrugged. 'Come in to tea. It'll give them a shock.'

It certainly did. She and Josh pretended quite smoothly that nothing had ever happened, and the confusion Hannah tried vainly to hide was fun to watch. Simon just grinned and said nothing. Sulis did her best to behave totally normally, but as she carried the dishes out afterwards she wondered what normal was, because she had always thought she had given nothing away before. Hannah took the tray. 'Have you . . . did you . . . um.'

The letter.

Sulis raised an eyebrow. 'What?'

Hannah said, 'Nothing. It's so nice to see Josh back! Um . . . Sulis, can I ask you . . . ?'

She smiled brightly. 'Got to go! Simon's got the keys to the cellars. We're finally going to explore the locked room.'

Hannah wound a lock of hair round her finger. 'Oh. Why does that remind me? Sulis, I rang you the other day on the office phone, but it's got some security block-thing on it. I forgot to say. I hope it didn't worry you.'

She stared. She saw her mobile shivering on the parapet of the roof. 'When?'

'The other day. I'm not sure. Are you OK?'

'Fine.' She was numb. Josh had been right. The man on the tourist bus had been no one.

At the door, Hannah's voice caught her. 'I hope you find out what's in the secret room,' she said quietly.

Sulis stopped. She looked back, but her foster-mother just stood there, against the sink, outlined against the light from the high window, her fair hair a frizzy cloud around her small face.

Downstairs, Simon had a torch and wore his oldest coat and boots. 'It'll be filthy in there, mind,' he said.

Josh shrugged. 'Can I carry anything?'

'Oh . . . yes. The spare light, please.' Simon had a camera with a tripod. He hefted it along the hall, down the stairs, and out of the front door. Sulis followed, thoughtful. She looked up and saw Hannah peeping down through the curtains. Well, at least the letter would never get sent. Hannah must suspect she'd read it. But she didn't care.

With a lot of trouble they got the camera down the steps into the courtyard. The evening was vaguely smoky, the sky twilight purple, blurred by the streetlamps. The cellars breathed a musty chill.

'Right.'

Simon looked up at the archway. 'First I'll take some shots of the stonework, and those initials. Stand back.'

He spent ages arranging the camera. Josh and Sulis stood and watched, not wanting to talk. The cellars were shadowy and cold, and she had the strangest feeling sometimes that there were more people there than the three of them, more shadows on the walls, but when the camera had finally clicked and whirred for the third time Simon said, 'OK. Fab. Now we open up.'

Josh grinned at Sulis.

The key didn't look like a key. It was a strange jointed thing with bits of metal sticking out from it everywhere. But Simon seemed to know how to use it.

'All-purpose opener, we call it. The lock is very rusty.'

It wouldn't even turn. He sprayed it with WD40 and tried again.

The metal rod moved and slid, and then he forced it round and they could hear the reluctant grinding of the mechanism. 'I don't think this has ever been opened.'

'Like Tutankhamun's tomb,' Josh said. 'Maybe we'll find treasure.'

She stood behind them, watching. A sort of panic was rising in her; she wanted to go back, go out, upstairs, into her room.

But she held herself still.

'OK. Now we've got it.' Simon pulled at the door; then he pushed it. It didn't move.

'Stuck. Give me a hand, Josh.'

Josh squeezed in next to him and they both put their shoulders to it. Sulis could feel the strain. She could feel the old timbers, stubborn and warped, fixed for years in their frame. She could feel the darkness behind,

220

the deep, untouched darkness, the
had broken since the door had been lo
centuries ago.

'Wait,' she gasped.

Still pushing, Josh twisted his head to her. 'Why

She didn't know why. There was no why.

They pushed harder and the door began to grate on its hinges, shuddering inwards. As it opened she stared with fascination and horror at the slot of blackness that widened, wrinkling her nose up at the musty stale air that wafted out, imagining it like a dark wave washing over her.

'Nearly. Just a bit more.'

Had they talked to Josh? Had they all discussed her, her obsessions, what she must have seen as a child? The terrible beauty of the girl falling into blue air?

'Just one more shove, Josh, near this side.'

Was there a conspiracy of silence against her?

'Thanks. Fantastic.' Simon gave the door a final heave and it juddered wide. He wiped filth from his hands. 'We're in! Right. Well. Here goes. Can I have the torch, Sulis, or do you want the honour?'

She glanced at him, and there was nothing but excitement in his face.

So she pushed past him, and clicked the torch on.

She shone its beam into the darkness.

Zac

We walked down to the baths together, I in my dark coat & Sylvia with a green cloak around her. In the gracious spaces of Queen's Square a few linkboys led groups of men toward the gaming houses; a carriage with outriders paraded solemnly by, the warmth from the horses' steamy backs touching my face.

But down in the insalubrious alleys the city stank. How could Forrest hope to change such a world as this? Stepping over a pile of muck I guided Sylvia under the overhanging roofs, through the noxious lanes, where a filthy pig snuffled in a trough.

She said, 'Are you sure about this, Zac?'

'I have to have the note-of-promise.' Didn't she see that? 'I have no money to pay these debts, Sylvia. My father is bankrupt. If I am ever to make anything of my wretched life . . .'

'Yes. Yes. All right. I see.'

Her arm was light on mine. Then she pulled it away,

drawing her cloak tighter. I said, 'You're afraid.'

'Not of Compton.'

'No? How well do you really know him?'

She wasn't looking at me. Dark thoughts came to me. Did she meet him in secret? Did they talk about me? I fought down a rising panic.

'I knew him when I worked at Gibson's. A little.'

'You never talk much about that place.'

She shrugged. 'It was a hellpit. People lost everything there. They were robbed, often. Once, one of the girls died.'

I stared. 'How?'

'She fell . . . I was there, I saw it. Things were dangerous for me after that. That was why I ran.'

'Someone pushed her . . . ?'

Her eyes flickered to mine, & then she looked away. 'Please, Zac. I don't want to talk about it.'

She was a girl of mystery still, then. But we were nearly at the baths, so I tapped the leather folder under her arm. 'Now. You have the plans. You know what to do.'

I had given her my forged designs at home; then she had slipped into Forrest's workroom with them for a moment & come out with this old folder, the designs placed neatly inside. I was surprised, but she had said she thought it would make them look more authentic, more as if she had stolen them. Now, glancing at a corner of paper that peeped out, I prayed that Compton would not guess at the subterfuge.

Seeing my glance, she tucked the paper in hastily.

'Shall I come in with you?' I asked.

'No.' She pulled the wide hood round her face. 'Watch if you want, but if he sees you it's all over, so keep well away.'

'Be careful,' I said. It was foolish, & sounded it. She smiled at me, her eyes lit with nerves. Then she hurried inside.

I waited five cold minutes before I followed her.

The baths, even at night, were loud with noise. Forrest often railed against the vulgarity of the place, & as the hot steam gathered around me I understood what he meant. The ancient pools & sacred springs were pits of noisome dirt. Filth crusted the steps, & the noise was deafening. There were even a few musicians, scraping rusty fiddles for coins. Men & women both, dressed in strange voluminous garments, waded & splashed, helped in & out by servants paid for the job. I dared not think what diseases most of them carried. Bladud's magic spring was wretched now indeed. Other servants waited at the common pump, clutching empty bottles to fill & take back for the master's gout or mistress's scrofula. The smell of sweating bodies was such that I had to fight the desire to take out my handkerchief & press it against my nose. Instead, I looked for Sylvia.

She was standing near the pump, the wallet held under her arm. I saw that the silk of her cloak was splashed & darkened by the water, but as I waited steam drifted between us, & a beggarwoman pestered me to buy trinkets from a tray of junk.

I told her to leave me alone.

When I looked up again, Compton was there.

I drew a breath. His lordship wore another elegant coat, & a silver-hilted sword. He pulled off his hat & bowed to her, mocking. I indulged myself with a dream of knocking him to the ground at my feet. It was a very pleasant thought.

There was an ancient pillar nearby, green with slime. I stood behind it & watched them. They talked. He was smiling & laughing. She was quick, quiet, agitated. She glanced round once or twice. For a moment she seemed almost to be pleading with him; his smile went & he said something hard & sharp. Then he caught her arm.

I stood rigid. I wanted to run out & fling him off. But I told myself to be still because both of us would have revenge on him this way.

She took out the leather folder. I saw his face light; he reached for it but she held it back, & I knew she was asking for my note-of-promise, because he laughed then, & glanced round, as if he guessed I was there.

All the air between us rippled with steam. A great splatter from the bath doused me with hot drops; they touched my cheek like the fingertips of a hand. As I wiped them away I saw Compton take something from his pocket & offer it to Sylvia, maliciously holding it from her fingers & dangling it before her, like a man does with titbits for his dog.

I felt my teeth grit.

But she took hold of it with a quick snatch, & read it. Then she put it into her pocket, & gave him the plans.

I held my breath. Because he untied the wallet & looked inside at once, his eyes alert. Suddenly I wondered if I had mis-gauged his knowledge. What if he recognized the errors, the impossible proportions? My drawings were good, my hand neat & as like my master's as I could make it. Surely he could not know.

He didn't . . .

He closed the folder & said something & she snapped an answer back. And then she was walking, away from him & away from me, her head down, thrusting people aside, pushing through the crowd. Compton turned & went out of the main door. Instantly I shouldered my way after Sylivia, slipping on the treacherous steps, hot in the clammy air of the sulphurous pools. She ran up the steps to street level.

'Sylvia!' I called her but she must not have heard, so I ran after her.

The street was cold after the steamy heat; its darkness was complete, but I could hear her feet, running ahead. I followed her into Bath Street, past the hospital, into the clutter of shops & lockups the carpenters use, the saw-close.

'Sylvia! Wait! Here I am.'

Ahead of me in the empty street, she stopped. She did not turn, but waited till I caught her up, & when I reached her side she did not look at me, but thrust a paper into my hands.

One small lamp flickered where a night-watchman sat. I ran to it & held the paper under it, & cried out in joy.

It was certainly my note-of-promise. There was my own signature, scrawled in despair across the sum. One hundred guineas. Payable to Lord Compton.

'You did it! You got it!' I wanted to swing her off her feet & kiss her, but when I turned she was standing apart from me, & her face was grave.

'Yes,' she said. 'I got it.'

Her coldness chilled me. So I bowed formally. 'Thank you, my lady.'

'It was nothing,' she said. There was a glimmer of water on her face, as if the steam had gathered there & trickled. I could not tell why she was so hard, almost angry with me. But the note was real enough & rustling in my hands, so I held its corner carefully to the flame in the sooty lamp & watched it catch light, the paper blackening at the edge & then suddenly crumpling into fire. I turned it carefully & watched my debt smoulder into ashes & fall at my feet. For good measure, I put my heel to the pieces & ground them into the dirt.

When it was done she walked away, & I went after her. 'I feel so free! Sylvia, you can't guess how the debt weighed on me!' Indeed, I only knew how much myself now, when it was gone. 'Things will be different now. I will work so hard! Forrest will barely know me. And my father – I will send him money. Every month! Half my salary.'

She was silent, walking beside me.

'And he had no idea? Compton? He was satisfied with the plans?'

'He was satisfied.'

'What a fool he is'

'Yes.' Her voice was flat. 'What a fool he is.'

Did she feel sorry at having outwitted him? I could not imagine it. We walked back quickly. She seemed disinclined to talk, as if the task of deceiving Compton had taken all the energy out of her. I fear I may have prattled on, because in my joy I did something I had not meant to do. I told her about the secret chamber in the heart of the Circus.

She listened intently. By the time we reached the house she knew it all, even my plans to watch the Oroboros meeting. She said, 'I'm coming with you.'

I tried to hide my dismay. 'Sylvia . . .'

She turned on me like a viper. 'I'm coming with you, & don't even think about stopping me! You've got your precious note, & you owe me for that! You're safe, & that's all that matters to you!' And she ran up the steps of the house & slammed the front door in my face.

I stared at the quivering black panels in bewilderment.

Now what had I done?

All next day I did not see her. She wasn't at breakast, nor supper, & Mrs Hill said she had taken to her bed & was unwell. Forrest frowned. 'Is there anything I can do?'

'Nothing, zirr, & don't you worry yourself about missy.' The housekeeper cleared the dishes. 'A case of the vapours, as I know full well. It will all pass off tomorrow.'

She was avoiding me. I knew it, but had no idea why. Girls are impossible to understand.

Forrest sat a while, musing, & I watched him. He had fallen into one of his strange moments of dream, & I wondered what he was thinking there, twirling the wineglass in his finger & thumb, what druid mysteries were perplexing him. Or was it something as practical as the materials for the broken scaffold? What a mixture he was!

I decided to try my luck. 'I will be going out about the town tonight, sir, if you allow.'

He looked up. 'What?'

'About the town.'

'Not gaming, Zac, I trust.'

I smiled, complaisant. 'I do not game, sir.'

'Good. It's a great folly.' He put the glass down. 'How do you think the work is going, Zac? Do you like what you see?'

I said, 'It will crown your life's endeavour.'

'A crown of acorns.' He smiled. 'But are you sure?' He fixed me with his dark eyes, always so quick. 'Or are you just appeasing your master's vanity?'

I did not know what to say. And then the words came out & I surprised myself. 'I believe the Circus will be spoken of in days to come as great architecture. I'm honoured to be involved with it.' And it was true.

He looked at me over the empty table. 'Are we friends, Zac?'

Now it was I who turned my glass. 'Yes,' I said.

He nodded. 'That pleases me. Sometimes I thought . . . because I know I am not an easy man to live with. Ideas rise up in my head like the bubbles in the spring. Who knows where they all come from? But I am glad you're working with me. I see a great future for you some day, Zac. Despite your airs & graces.'

I laughed, though the final sentence irked me just a little. But his mention of the bubbling spring reminded me of the hidden chamber, & I told myself that he had not shared this with me, & so how much was his friendship worth?

He rose. 'I have to go out too, later. Enjoy your evening, Zac. Let's hope Sylvie will be back with us tomorrow.'

I watched him go out & up the stairs.

Sylvie. That was what Compton called her.

I spent the intervening hours in my room, all hung about with my clothes. I tried to study, but at just before eleven the front door shut softly & I jumped up to the window & looked out. Forrest's dark shadow slipped into the street.

I grabbed my coat & crept past Sylvia's door but it opened & she came out at once, as if she had been sitting there on the bed, waiting. This time her cloak was black.

'He's just left,' I said.

She nodded.

'Are you really ill?'

She looked at me strangely. 'I don't know yet.'

We tiptoed down the stairs & out of the house. Mrs Hall was gone home – just as well, because I dared not imagine what she might think.

So for the second night in a row Sylvia & I walked the streets of the city, but something had changed between us now; she did not give me her arm & we said hardly anything until we came to the edge of the site & saw Forrest not far ahead of us, tall & shadowy in his old coat.

The half-built facade cast a long shadow over the huts & masonry, the scaffolding & stacked stone. Looking up, I saw the moon was full, glinting on pools of water & the metal edges & corners of struts. But the centre of the Circus was an inky darkness, & as Sylvia moved in front of me I almost stumbled to the floor. She grabbed my wrist tight.

Forrest paused.

He glanced around, & we stood frozen. For a moment

I knew he would call out, 'Is that you, Zac?' & I would have to answer him. But he seemed to turn, & then was gone, into the cellars.

Sylvia's lips were warm at my ear. 'Keep close to me.'

I intended to. She seemed to see in the dark like a cat; she led me through the rubble of the site.

There was no sign of the watchman. And the others of the Oroboros must have come as secretly; there were no horses or carriages in the half-made street.

We hesitated at the entrance to the cellar.

Sylvia withdrew her hand. 'Well. Are you sure you want to do this?'

'It's too late to go back.'

She looked at the dark doorway. 'No it isn't.'

'You don't have to come.'

She seemed to smile sadly in the dark. 'No I don't.' But she didn't move away. Instead I heard her sigh, & she whispered, 'Are we really saving him, Zac? Or betraying him?'

I had no answer to that. Instead I edged past her & slipped into the cellar.

It was bitterly cold, & as we went down it seemed deeper than in the daylight, as if we descended through time. The bare walls exhaled a noxious damp; I saw my breath fog the air as I inched through the dark.

The pile of wood rose in front of us like a screen. I paused, listening anxiously for voices, but the shadows ahead were quiet. I dared not speak to Sylvia now; the room would have echoed our murmurs. And the foggy night had crept in after us so that I could barely see her.

I reached out & touched the wood. It was icy, the rough grain catching on my fingers. I eased myself to the end of it & peered round.

The arch & passageway were black.

Then, as I stared, a flame sputtered to life in the secret room. I saw nothing but the flame; it was carried down by an unseen hand & touched to a wick.

The flame steadied & grew. Yellow light flickered in the chamber. I saw the bare walls, lined with shadows. I saw the pool, faint steam rising from it. A bubble rose to the surface & plipped, silently.

The flame moved. From candle to candle it went, until there was a ring of light about the water. Vast ripples of shadow slid down the walls. The darkness crackled & murmured.

They must be there already. The men of the Oroboros, the secret cult that I knew nothing of. Were they men of power in the city: lords, councillors, merchants, the great and the good? Was Ralph Alleyn among them, or Greye? Or were they antiquarians like Forrest, men who dreamed of druids & lost gods, who elaborated foolish theories in great books that no one read?

I could not see. I was at the very edge of the wooden screen & I still could not see.

Sylvia's grip was tight, but I pulled away. I stepped across to the archway, a brief instant in the light, crept into the passage & flattened myself against the stones there, my heart thudding in my chest.

And then I took a breath, & peered into the chamber.

Bladud

Beyond the world's orbit is darkness. We live in the light of the moon and the sun, of torches and candles. We fear what lies outside our warm ring.

But druids and wise men need to know. We need to know how the darkness sometimes creeps inside us, how we let it in. Fear, betrayal, dread. These are the mysteries of time, that snake that eats its own tail.

I remember I climbed my tower in the early morning and looked out from its top. I could see a long way, as far as the downs. I could see the day's beginning, and in the west, I could see the place it would end. Because the day is a circle too.

I fitted the wings to my back and I spread them wide.

My heart leapt with fear as the breeze nudged me. My feet were at the very edge of the stonework; the feathers all rustled and moved with the energy they held.

Once before I had been in a place between life and death. Now I was there again.

I leapt into the blue sky. I screamed.

Sulis

There was a passageway, and at its end, a chamber.

In the chamber was nothing but some sort of circular feature in the centre.

The walls were bare stone. Simon said, 'Well. No treasure, then.'

They stood, looking around.

Sulis was disappointed, as if she had expected some message from Forrest here, some object left by him. The roof was dim above her; she flashed the torch over it and they saw the carefully corbelled rings of stone.

'What was it for?' Josh muttered.

'Good question.' Simon went out for the camera and carried it in. 'There's nothing to tell us.'

Their voices rang as if they were deep inside a shaft, or as if the great facade above the ground contained them, even down here. Sulis crouched down over the central circle.

'There's this. It's a pool. Or it was.'

Even now the earth looked damp. She put her hand down and felt it; there was a faint but real warmth, and her fingers sank into a soft mud studded with tiny gritty stones.

Simon bent and stared. 'A hot spring? That's quite remarkable.'

She felt the warmth in her fingertips. Something made her dig deeper; she scraped her fingers deep leaving five gouges that slowly filled, as she watched, with water that seeped up from the depths of the earth.

'Forrest must have known it was here.' Simon was excited now. 'Perhaps it was the reason he even chose the site for his Circus. I'm sure no one else knows anything about this.' He glanced round. 'We should really get some geofizz down here, you know. There could be all sorts of stuff underneath.' He flashed the torch into the darkness; the light ghosted over something pale.

'There,' Josh said. 'What's that?'

The torch refocused, searching. Sulis turned hers that way too. Both beams met, and converged, and stopped.

They lit a square stone. It stood by itself, placed deliberately on the bare floor.

It had been smoothed and on its side an image was carved, unweathered, still fresh from the workmen's chisels. Simon drew in a deep breath.

Then he looked at Sulis.

237

She was still, unable to move.

'What is it?' Josh muttered.

'A metope.' Simon's voice was low. 'An extra one, it seems. One they didn't use on the Circus.'

Sulis stepped forward. She brought the torch beam up close to the image, crouched down in front of it, ran the light over its crumbling edges, its sharp smooth surface.

It showed a winged figure, arms wide, plunging earthwards.

'Icarus,' Josh said.

Simon shrugged. 'More probably Bladud. Forrest was fascinated with the local legend. Some say he even imagined himself to be Bladud, in some strange way. Bladud made himself wings. He threw himself off some temple and tried to fly.'

Sulis touched the stone. She was closer to it than they were. Her eyes were near to the grainy golden stone, the stone of the city, hacked from the downs in Ralph Alleyn's quarry, hauled here and cut into this image. She could see that the winged figure had long hair.

Was it a man? Or was it a girl?

Josh was next to her. He was saying, 'Are you OK, Sulis?'

She couldn't answer him. Instead she said, 'What happened to him? The druid?'

Simon stood up, his knees creaking. 'He was smashed to pieces, the book said.'

She had known that. And in the shadows behind her, in the dark spaces of the chamber, she knew someone else was standing. It wasn't Simon or Josh. She knew who it was.

The smell told her. It made her gasp with memory. The smell of dead leaves and soil, the smell of mustiness, or rain-soaked clothes. She turned her head slowly, and saw him near the door, but he already had his back to her. He walked behind Josh and Simon and he made no sound and neither of them saw him go. He walked through the stone archway and didn't look back.

She scrambled up. 'I've got to go. To get some air.'

'Sulis . . .'

She was past them, pushing past. She threw the torch to Josh and he grabbed it before it smashed; then she was running, through the chamber and under the arch, back into the cellar. A shadow moved before her, perhaps her own, perhaps another girl's, running and laughing, and in front of them both the stranger paced.

As she ran out into the sunken courtyard the night was a swirling fog, the moon a silver disc like a coin spun somewhere above it.

She raced up the steps and stopped halfway.

He was here.

He was fumbling at the door of the house – her house. As she froze in the dimness she saw how he pulled out a key and pushed it into the lock. Then he turned it, and the door opened and he went inside.

She stared at the closed black panels in disbelief.

Then she walked up the steps, and followed him in.

The hallway looked normal, though some of the fog seemed to have slid in. The man was running up the stairs, his tread heavy, his breath wheezy. He was already out of sight round the turn of the bannister.

'Wait!' she hissed. 'Don't go up there!'

Hannah was there, on her own. Sulis raced up, as quietly as she could. Surely he was only just ahead! But as she turned each landing the steps were always further away, his shadow huge and distorted on the wall above, until she came to the door of the flat and found it ajar.

She walked quietly down the corridor.

'Hannah?'

The living room was empty, the radio singing faintly to itself. From the bedroom she could just hear Hannah's voice, chatting on the phone. Maybe to Alison. Sulis looked round.

The small door to the attic stair was open.

She ran up, and stopped outside her room.

A sound fluttered inside.

She waited, her forehead against the door, trying to identify it. A soft, crackling flutter. A thud.

She glanced back, hoping Josh had followed her, but there was no one there, and she knew she was quite alone in this, as she had been since that day she and Caitlin had run away and taken the bus to the park.

She turned the handle.

Her room was pale and quiet, the bed neatly made, her clothes in a pile on the chair. No sign anyone was here. But as she watched, a thud on the window made her jump, and then a vivid flash of darkness slashed past her, so that she gasped and jumped back, letting the door slam in her shock.

There was a bird in the room.

It flew in the corners of her eyes, in the slants of moonlight. It fluttered against the mirror, the cornice. It made the coat hanging on the door sway and fall.

It cracked against the window like a stone.

She had to let it out.

Carefully, terrified it would tangle in her hair and peck her eyes, she edged into the room, past the bed to the window. The latch was down; she forced it back and as she did so the bird squawked past her and she glimpsed it, a black, jagged flight, crazy with fear.

She grabbed the casement and tugged it open. Night air hit her face with coolness. She turned. 'It's open. Go on. Go out.'

The window yawned wide. Suddenly the room was silent; she stood breathless, the night air blowing her hair in her eyes.

Was there a bird?

Because the room was silent and she was no longer sure about anything any more.

And then like an arrow it burst from the mirror and slashed past her, out into the dark, and she saw it

241

zigzag on to the wide roof.

She climbed after it, through the window to the base of the great stone acorn that rose into the sky. Below lay the Circus, quiet in the mist, its streetlamps hazy, the great trees at its centre masses of uneasy shadow.

'Sulis.'

She turned.

He was sitting on the tiles of the roof. His coat was bunched up behind him like wings. He said, 'Remember me, Sulis?'

Her heart thudded. She said, 'You've found me.'

'I found you a long time ago. But you'd never listen to me, Sulis. You kept running away from me. Other people, other towns. It was only when you came here I knew I could speak to you. Because this is my place.'

His face was marked with leprosy and scars and dirt. His breath wheezed in the air. His eyes were brown and steady.

She said, 'Josh doesn't believe in you. He says you weren't there – in the museum. Or in the street or the bus.'

'Maybe he's right.'

She shook her head. 'Are you going to push me off, like you pushed Caitlin?'

Did he smile? 'I didn't push Caitlin. You know that.'

'I saw you.' She turned and faced him, and the words built up in her and poured out. 'You've always been in my life since that day. You were the one who ruined my

242

life. It would have all been so different without you.'

'Caitlin ruined your life.'

She stared at him, amazed. 'Caitlin was my friend.'

'Was she? Are you sure?'

Of course she was sure. And yet, as soon as he said it, she wasn't. It was as if he had focused a light on something never thought about, always assumed to be true.

'You remember.' He lifted a winged arm, and pointed. 'There she is.'

A ghost of a girl, standing with her back to Sulis, leaning precariously out over the parapet. The faintest outline on the night.

Sulis was cold. Her fingers were chilled.

'If she was your friend, call her. She'll turn round. You'll see her again.'

She couldn't move. Her lips were dry.

She didn't want to say the name. She didn't want to see the girl turn. *She didn't want to see her face*.

A voice said, 'Sulis? Where are you?'

Hannah. And Josh. Instantly she ducked inside, ran to the door of her room and locked it, jamming the key round seconds before someone knocked on it, hard.

'Su? Are you all right?'

She stepped back, breathless. 'I'm fine.'

'Simon said you ran off so fast . . .'

'I'm fine. I'm just . . . changing.'

'Josh is here.'

'I know. Five minutes. That's all.'

She backed away, climbed back outside. The mist was drifting like faint drizzle, blurring the lights.

He hadn't gone. His sleeves were pulled over his hands, as if he was cold. He turned his head, his eyes attentive as a jackdaw's. 'Tell me about Caitlin,' he said.

She sat on the sill. 'We played together. We built towers and houses.'

'Together?'

'Sort of together.'

'You mean you built them.'

'Yes.' Sulis nodded, remembering. 'I built them. I always wanted to play with those blocks, but she didn't. She said they were boring. Once I built a really high tower, and she knocked it down.'

Why had she forgotten that? 'And she made me walk home with her. Every night after school. It was miles out of my way but she didn't care. She laughed.'

He looked out at the trees. 'You could have said no.'

'I couldn't. She . . . was stronger than me. I did what she said.' Now she let herself remember, and the ghostly girl sitting on the parapet seemed to become more solid, the breeze stirring her hair. 'When she was there I was smaller and quieter. I was her shadow.'

He preened a sudden feather into the dark. 'We're all shadows.'

Sulis was stunned. What door had she unlocked to let this out? Because in all the years since Caitlin's death she had never let herself think it.

'The running away?' he whispered.

'It was her idea. I didn't want to go. She dragged me.'
She remembered Caitlin's hand on hers, the hissed fierce
whisper. *Stay then. I don't care. I'll just never speak to
you ever again*. The running after. The pleading. The
words were hot, humiliating.

'Su!' Josh's voice. A rattle at the bedroom door.
She ignored it.

The stranger slid down the roof towards her. His face
was healing now, the leprosy fading as she looked. His
eyes were brown and deep. He said, 'But you went. On
the bus. To the park.'

'Oh but I cried. All the time. I wanted to go home. I
was scared. She just kept saying, *Shut up. It'll be fine.
We'll show them* . . . I hated her.' She raised her eyes to
his, and whispered it, a hiss of venom on the night. '*I
hated Caitlin*.'

'Su. Please open the door!'

She turned but his voice stopped her. 'And
the stranger?'

She stood in the mist and her arms were around
herself and she could say it. 'No one came up the tower
with us. Not that tramp. Not you. Not anyone.'

He smiled, satisfied.

'It was her idea to climb the tower. She pushed me up
in front of her. We got to the top and she was laughing
at me. Messing around. Saying she could do anything.

She could fly. She sat on the edge, her feet dangling. I said, 'Get up, come away from the edge.' I begged her. But she wouldn't.'

The ghost girl was real now. The pink quilted anorak. The woolly hat. The two blonde plaits.

Sulis stared at her. 'Caitlin stood up and she spread her arms. Look, she's doing it now. Can you see her?'

'I can see.'

'She had my wrist. I had to get away from her. She was pulling me. I was screaming.'

'You fought.'

'We struggled.'

'You bit . . .'

'. . . and kicked.'

'You pulled.'

'I screamed.'

He was right beside her. There was a great thudding going on somewhere, and voices down in the park, and a torch flickering over her. She said, 'They were all shouting. And then she stood up on the edge.'

'Just to show you . . .'

'. . . she could do it. Just to show me . . .'

'. . . she was stronger.'

The ghost girl climbed and balanced. She wobbled. Beside her a bird took off, fluttering into the dark with a harsh squawk. Sulis reached out. 'My hand. Look, here it is. Did I do it? Did I push her off? *Did I kill her?* Was I the stranger?'

There was no answer. Her hand moved closer, closer to the pink quilted coat, because she was afraid that Caitlin would turn, that she would see her face again, after all these years. But her hand moved as if she couldn't control it, inching forward, flat against the silky cloth between the shoulder blades.

Until Simon unlocked the door and said breathlessly, 'Su? Everything OK?'

Zac

What had I expected?

A circle of men in druid garb? Unholy & secret ceremonies? The sacrifice of some village girl with a golden sickle?

Something like that.

And maybe something like that had happened, because the chamber was dim with a faint mist, as if the men had been there only moments since, but had gone now, to shadows, to nothing.

Forrest was alone.

He sat waiting, by the spring, his coat bunched up on the ground. He said, 'Zac. Sylvia. Come in.'

For a moment I had the stupid idea of bolting back home to bed & pretending I had not been anywhere near this place. But Sylvia moved past me, & her dress rustled, & so I had to follow her, feeling so shamefaced & foolish I could scarely breathe.

He had lit the circle of candles, & they smouldered.

In their light I saw the spring; surrounding it another ring, of small, brown ovoids scattered on the earth. I trod on one by accident, & it crushed under my foot. I bent & looked at them.

They were acorns.

Forrest said, 'I'm afraid you've missed our little ceremony, Zac.'

I could not tell how angry he was. There was a great weight on him, but it seemed as much sorrow as wrath. Beside me, Sylvia was trembling.

I said, 'Sir, we were . . .'

'Curious?'

'Yes. Nothing more.'

He laughed, a dry, mirthless sound. He said, 'I do not object to curiosity. But I thought I had deserved better of you than this.'

At first I did not understand. Then he lifted one of the candles & moved it closer to him, & the light fell on something spread on the floor, a wide unfolded plan, held down at the corners by pieces of golden stone.

He looked up at me, across it. 'What is this mockery, Zac?' he whispered.

For a moment my mind was as dark as the chamber. And then Sylvia made some small sound, the very whisper of dismay. And it was as if a shaft of light had broken in, & suddenly I understood everything, understood that the plan in front of him was the one I had drawn, the grotesque warped copy of his work. *And that she had given the real plan to Compton.*

I could not move.

Even to breathe was impossible.

I looked at her; one glimpse. Her eyes were fixed on me. Her face was white as chalk.

It was only a fraction of an instant. And yet I seemed to see all my life in that time – the years of my apprenticeship lost, the buildings I would never design now – & hers too; seemed to see her begging on the London road, losing herself in that filthy city of darkness. She had betrayed all of us. Why should I save her?

Yet I pulled myself upright, adjusted my sleeve & said nothing.

Forrest touched the plan. 'Where is the original?'

'Sold,' I muttered.

'To Compton?'

I bowed. Words would only fail me.

He shook his head, as if he was too moved to speak. His voice was choked with bitterness. 'You owed him gambling debts?'

'Master Alleyn told you?'

'He hinted. But, Zac, why didn't you come to me?' He was on his feet now, facing me, his words torn from him, harsh & raw. 'Was I so forbidding a master? Did I deserve this!'

Beside me, Sylvia stood like a shadow in the chamber. She did not speak or look at me. I was sore with anger; I wanted to shout at her, to him, 'She did it! This lying girl you took in & preferred to me!'

But I just shook my head.

He took up the plan & threw it in my face. 'And you insult me with this! I could have forgiven you the debts, Zac, even giving away the secrets of my work, but to seek to subvert it! To have the men build this crippled ruin . . . to destroy me. That I cannot ever understand.' He stood close to me, & his eyes were black. 'Building is magic, Zac. It is our high art. It must never be betrayed.'

Sylvia gave a great choking sob.

For a moment of brief joy I thought then that she'd tell him, that she'd confess, but she didn't. She turned & pushed past me, running away into the darkness of the tunnel.

Forrest stepped back. He drew his hand over his face, pushed back his tangled hair. Then he turned away. 'I can't even bear to look at you. Go now, sir. Go to the house, pack your things & leave. Don't be there when I get back. Our partnership is ended.'

There were many things I could have said. My face was red with humiliation, & yet I was proud, & though that pride burned me like venom I hugged it to myself & lifted my head & turned on my heel as coolly as I could. But as I walked away from him through the darkness I walked into a terrible remorse, & it was all I could do not to turn & tell him what the girl had done.

Because I would be leaving her in his house, like a

viper coiled round his life.

I stopped. 'Sir, please . . .'

'*Go, Zac!*' It burst out of him like a cry. And so I went.

Outside, the night was a ghostly chill of mist. There seemed more lights than usual on the site, but they were mere nebulas of paleness. My breath smoked around me.

I walked through the piles of stone without looking to right or left. What would become of me? Why was I throwing away my life for a girl who could do such a thing as this to us? For a slut off the streets who cared not a jot for me?

I stopped. I would go back & force him to hear.

If she was thrown out, what should I care?

'Zac.'

She was standing in the doorway of one of the finished houses.

I stared at her through the dimness. I said, 'What have you done! I trusted you, Sylvia! I . . .'

'Have you told him? Did you tell him?'

I shook my head. She gave a small groan. 'You must. You have to . . .'

'I will not,' I said loftily. All my resolutions of a moment ago were gone; I was Master Peacock again.

She put both hands to her face. 'Then I will.'

'No.' I crossed to her quickly, between the piled stones. 'You'll end up on the streets.'

'I deserve it.'

252

I did not want to disagree. Instead I asked, 'What hold does Compton have on you?'

'The same as he had on you.' She shook her head. 'Do you think the women at Gibson's don't gamble? I owed him more than you. He planned all of it, once he knew where I was. I had no choice.' She was not crying. Her face was drawn & white.

'Yes you did.'

'People like us aren't free, Zac. I tried to run away, many times. I was afraid. And now I've betrayed Forrest. I'd give my life for him, do you know that? And yet I can still do this.'

I was silent.

For a moment all the city around us seemed still; the dark shoulders of the downs, the huddle of clustered houses below. Then a dog barked somewhere & Sylvia said, 'Don't leave. Go back to the house, & when he comes there, tell him the truth. Tell him everything.'

'But what about you?'

'Forget about me. I'll move on. I have my clothes, some money. I'll be fine.' She laughed, a brittle merriment. 'There's always another city. It may not be the perfect one Forrest wants to build, but it will have to be enough for me. Goodbye, Zac Peacock.'

I could not smile. Instead I nodded. I wanted to say more but she turned & ducked into the building.

I waited, but she didn't come back.

When I turned away there was an instant when I felt

lost; the familiar chaos of the site suddenly disorienting, the enclosing facade too complete, as if the thirty houses of the Circus had sprouted up out of our imaginations, & stood here now like great stones of a henge, as witnesses of my folly. I stood uncertain, thinking for a moment there were trees in front of me; five tall trees in the heart of the site, their branches snagged against the moon. And then a bird flew flapping past me, & I glanced up to watch it.

I saw her.

She had climbed up through the ladders & scaffolding of the house, right up to the parapet of the roof. Her dress was pale & it shimmered in the moonlight; she was leaning over the stonework, her hands grasping the newly cut slabs. She looked down into the cluttered spaces of the site.

My breath caught in my throat.

Forrest came out of the cellar. I yelled, 'Master!'

He turned quickly, stared where I pointed. There was a moment of utter silence. Then we were both running; he reached the house first, & I heard him thundering up the stairs & leaping for the ladders that led to the higher floors.

Behind him, I threw myself up. My hands slid on grease. Clouds of stonedust fell on me like a golden snow. The bannisters ended in midair; I found the ladder & hauled myself on to its rungs, my breath gone, my heart pounding.

At the top for a moment everything was black before my eyes; strange spots swam & dizzied me. Staggering, I edged along the scaffolding to the roof.

'Sylvie.' Forrest was ahead, in the dark, his breath nothing but a cracked wheeze. 'Please. Don't do this.'

I stopped behind him.

She was sitting with her legs through the gap. In places the roof was a mere skeleton of trusses; orderly rows of upright stone slates stood ready for laying. Spaces a man could fall through yawned in the dark.

Forrest could hardly breathe; I heard the painful gasp of his chest. 'Sylvia?'

Her voice came from far away. 'Don't blame Zac. It was me.'

He fought to breathe. I moved, but there was no way past him on the narrow platform.

She said, 'Compton wanted the plans. He told me to get them. I owed him money, & . . . there were other things. I'd known him at Gibson's . . .'

'You loved him?' Forrest whispered.

I saw her turn; her eyes were dark in her ghostly face. 'Maybe I thought I did, once. He was fine & handsome & he said things . . . but I soon came to see what he was. His cruelty. His sneering ways. But I could never get free of him. He was always there.'

She shrugged, a despairing movement. 'I hate him, & I can't break free of him. It's as if he's stronger than me, that he just has to look, or say something, and I do it.' She stared out at the misty night. 'Zac wanted to give him the fake plans. But I knew he'd find out what they were, sooner or later, & come after me. Even if it was years, he'd come, because he would enjoy finding me. And so I tricked both of you.'

Forrest said, 'It doesn't matter . . .'

'Of course it matters.' She turned, furious. 'You gave me a life, & I betrayed you.'

His voice was hoarse. 'Yes. But if you jump from there you'll betray me again, & for ever, Sylvia. We will never be able to change that. In all our lives, Zac's & mine, that image will be there, of you, leaping out. We'll see it when we sleep.' He edged closer. 'And my work . . . my building . . . will be flawed. You will have ruined it.'

Did he know that would make her smile? Because it did, a watery, rueful smile.

'Always your building.'

'Always.' He knelt, stretching out his hand to her. The planks creaked.

She saw me behind him. She said, 'Haven't I already done that?'

'No. The design is mine. Let Compton copy it. Let him be famous for it. That doesn't matter.' He wheezed out a laugh. 'Because the Circus will stand & that is all that matters. I designed it for us. We three, the points of the triangle.'

He coughed. His whole body quivered with a gasp for air. I crouched quickly, because I knew this was his plan,

256

that an asthma attack would bring her hurrying in to help him. I grabbed his arm & bent low.

'She's coming. I'm sure.'

She was; her dress caught on the wood & she tore it, angrily. Forrest had his face down, away from me; I felt his fierce convulsive struggle for air; his fingers tore at the wood & his chest heaved & then he slumped against me.

I looked up at her, the first fear striking deep into me.

'It's real! He's really . . .'

She had his arms; we held him up. He gasped & struggled for breath as if it was a demon he fought with, as if the very air was his enemy, his face flushed, his eyes staring into a darkness we could not see. And he was right, because I will never forget that fight for life, that terrible wheezing, the grip of his hand in mine, so hard it hurt, his nails cutting my palm.

The sudden loosening of his fingers.

The silence.

I held him till I was sure there was no more struggle in him, nothing left to happen, no overworked heart still to beat. Sylvia was sobbing uncontrollably, but I could not cry or even feel anything, as I laid him carefully down on the wooden planks & felt all the strength go out of me too.

I was shaking, & I reached out my hand for her & she took it.

Somehere above us a bird flapped away, into the night.

Bladud

How can I tell you about the ecstasy of flight?!
To be free of the drag of the earth, to be free and high in the
blue sky! Never being pulled down, or having to fear that you
will fall!
There will be many stories about me. Those who like their
tales grim and realistic will say I plummeted to earth, and
was smashed to pieces on the stones. Like Icarus I flew too
high. Like Lucifer I rebelled and was too proud.
But the dreamers and the poets will have different versions.
They will say I flew away to strange lands, that I became a
bird and haunt the city still, that I return sometimes in
human form.
You will have to decide which is true for yourself, and what
truth means.
Beyond the circle are the heavens and the stars, the secrets of
which only the druids know . . .
You cannot go further yet.
You must stop now, and look around you, and understand.

The Circle will help you.
The Circle is the oldest magic.

Sulis

They were in the car.

Simon drove, and Hannah sat in the front passenger seat wearing a scarf and sunglasses, trying to look like an actress in some Fifties film. They had left the city and crossed the downs, the sun glorious in the sky and all the trees shedding their last golden leaves.

Sulis and Josh sat in the back. Neither of them had brought music, or anything to do. They both just sat and listened to Hannah's chat, and looked out of opposite windows at the green fields, and ocasionally at each other.

Hannah said, 'You two are very quiet.'

'We're fine,' Josh had said.

And they were.

Sulis stared at her reflection, slanted in the sun. The dye was beginning to fade out of her hair; the roots were copper, and she had stopped straightening it; it was back to a soft wave and it made her look different.

She wore a zany blue and green T-shirt and a new jacket Hannah had bought for her.

She felt like a shape-shifter.

'Not far now.' Simon changed gear and turned off the main road. 'I'm telling you, you'll love it. Very strange place. Forrest came here and surveyed the whole thing.'

'And if we don't love it,' Hannah said sweetly, 'we'll find the pub.'

Josh said, 'Sounds good.'

The lane was narrow, with high hedges on each side. Jackdaws rose from bare elm branches.

After crossing a narrow bridge and passing a toll house they drove through a tiny village and pulled up in a car park behind some houses.

When the engine stopped the silence surged back.

Hannah lowered her window. 'Just listen to that.'

Sheep. They baahed and cropped the field quietly. Sulis opened the door and got out.

'So where is it?'

'Right here.' Simon was dragging his camera from the boot. He pulled out boxes and a tripod and some books and a rug.

Sulis and Hannah looked at each other. Then Hannah grinned. 'You two go on. I'll carry all this junk with him. You'd think it was an expedition to the Sahara, not Stanton Drew.'

Josh opened the gate and he and Sulis walked

through. They walked side by side down a track to a stile and she climbed over it, leaving him to pick up a leaflet from the tourist box.

She sat on the top of the gate and looked at the circles.

They were incredibly old. The Great Circle spread out over the field and the sheep grazed and snoozed around the stones, so that they almost looked like a random scatter, but when she climbed down and walked towards them, up the slight slope, she saw the ring. It rose up around her, great slabs and boulders, some fallen, some skewed, some not there at all.

'It's not just one circle.' Josh was reading the leaflet. 'There were actually three. That's a smaller one, over there. With stones like avenues leading off. It says here . . .'

'Don't read about it! Look at it.'

It lay in a low valley. All around the hills and downs encircled them.

He shoved the leaflet in his pocket and they walked silently between the stones, the sheep moving reluctantly aside, or standing and staring at them, mouths chewing.

Where the smaller circle was a great stone had fallen. Sulis sat on it. Josh put his foot up and looked round, hands in pockets.

'So what's so great?'

'Don't ask me. It was Simon's idea.' She grinned. 'He

said I need to get out and see some countryside and have some fresh air.'

Josh nodded. They watched as Simon and Hannah carried the camera to the gate and went back for more stuff. Then he said, 'You weren't going to jump off that roof, were you?'

'Of course I wasn't.' She pulled on the fingers of her woolly gloves.

'Then why . . .'

'There was a bird trapped in my room. I had to get it out.' She had no intention of telling him all of it, because she no longer knew what had happened to her. In the last few days, the more she had thought of it the vaguer it had seemed – the voices her own, the stranger just a shadow on the roof, the girl a blur of her imagination. All she knew was that she was free. For the first time since Caitlin had fallen, she was free.

'What sort of bird?'

She didn't answer. Instead she said, 'Listen, Josh. I've remembered. I've remembered everything that happened.'

He waited.

She said, 'You were right. There never was a stranger. I see that now. I don't know why I couldn't think clearly before . . . it's as if my own mind grew a sort of hard scar over what happened, and it hurt to touch it.'

'And now it's healed?'

'I think so.' She looked at him. 'I've remembered

about Caitlin.'

Across the field, Simon set up the camera.

'She wasn't so much of a friend, was she?' Josh said.

Sulis stared at him in surprise. 'No, she wasn't. How did you guess that? She was a spiteful little bully. I was really under her thumb.' She was silent a moment, looking out at the stones. Then she said, 'I suppose after she died I didn't want to think about her like that. In my mind she became the friend I'd always wanted, sort of bright and sparky and full of ideas. I changed her.'

'Su . . . if there was no stranger . . .'

'What happened on the tower?' She nodded. 'That was all hidden too. Inside me. Inside and underneath.' She looked up. 'But now I think I know.' She took a deep breath, because this was hard. 'We climbed up the tower because Caitlin wanted to. I didn't. I was terrified and I just wanted to go home. But she dragged me halfway and then I went the rest of the way by myself, because I just had to go where she told me. It sounds stupid, but . . .'

'No it doesn't.'

Sulis nodded. 'Well, on the roof, she stood on the edge. Too near the edge. She was always daring, chancing her luck, showing off. She made me stand there too. And then she wobbled. We . . . my hand went out.'

She was still so long Josh whispered, 'You pushed her?'

Had she?

For a minute all the years of fear came back. But she said, 'No. I didn't. It was just . . . all so panicky. I was screaming and she was unsteady and I was terrified we'd both go over. So I dragged myself away. I didn't push her. I'm sure of that now. But I think for a long time – for years – I wasn't sure. So I let the stranger take the blame.'

'But all that time, Sulis. All those foster-homes, those sightings . . .'

She stared at him. 'Yes, but don't you see, I believed in him, Josh! He was real to me. I was really terrified he'd find me.'

They both sat in the quiet field. She wondered what he thought of her, but she was too relieved to worry. They watched as Simon took his careful photographs, aligning the stones with the horizon, with the trees.

'Stand there, both of you. And *smile*, Su!'

She hesitated. There was only one photograph, of a child frozen in the flashlight. But Josh grabbed her hand and they both stood there awkward, posing, and Simon clicked the camera and said, 'Cool,' and they laughed at him.

She looked at the image on the screen. A calm, older Sulis gazed back at her, Josh grinning next to her. Behind them, the stones circled.

Simon got out his surveying stuff – the tapes and computer and theodolite. 'Right. Time to work.

Give me a hand, you two.'

It took over an hour to survey the site. At the beginning they were all giggling and getting caught up in the tape, but as time went on Sulis got bored and she was sure Hannah was too. So they got the food from the car, and a rug, and set up under the fallen oak tree on the side of the site.

'Look at this.' Hannah waved at it. 'Must have been a huge tree once. Really ancient.'

The white trunk was bleached and seamed like driftwood. One whole side had all but broken off; it lay crashed to the ground, as if lightning had struck it, decades ago.

Sulis leaned against the splintered boughs, eating a sandwich. Above her, the sky was blue and empty.

Hannah said, 'Is everything all right, Su?'

'Everything's fine.'

'So . . . you'll be staying with us.'

Sulis turned. 'Why shouldn't I?'

'I just thought . . . with uni . . . And things have been a bit, tricky. You settling in, I mean.'

Sulis smiled, remembering the lost letter to Alison. She said firmly, 'I love staying with you and Simon. I love the Circus. Honestly.'

Hannah seemed relieved and pleased. 'I knew it. We're getting just like a family.'

Sulis laughed. She rolled over and lay on the rug, watching Josh and Simon trudge across.

Simon threw himself down. 'What a place. What a site. Look at this.' He turned the laptop for them to see. 'Jonathan Forrest's survey overlaid with the modern readings. He was accurate to within three centimetres. The man was a genius.'

'Eat some sandwiches.' Hannah pushed the packets over. 'Those are egg and those are cheese. The hummus is for me.'

Later, when Simon and Hannah had gone for walk, hand in hand, Josh sipped Coke from a can and said absently, 'Guess what. I'm going to uni.'

Sulis stared at him in astonishment. 'What?'

'Not pleased?'

'Of course I'm pleased, stupid. But I thought . . .'

'Simon's arranged it. He's all right, isn't he? There's some grant I can apply for – he's got the forms for me. He seems to think it's a certainty. It won't be that much money but probably enough to live on. Maybe they'll let me work part-time at the baths as well.' He leaned on his knees and stared out at the stones. 'Did you know that there was a ground radar survey done here in the Nineties and they found all sorts of weird stuff? There are circles of post holes out there under the grass. Nine concentric circles. Maybe four hundred oak pillars. As if some vast wooden building was once here, its centre open to the sky.'

'How old?'

'Neolithic. It was some important place. And now it's

268

all hidden, and forgotten.'

She said, 'I think you'll be a great archaeologist, Josh.'

'And I think you'll be a great architect.'

They laughed.

'Sulis! Time to go.' Hannah was running back across the field.

Sulis rolled off the rug and picked it up, tipping Josh on to the muddy grass. He put his hand down and picked up a handful of litter from the sheep-gnawed turf.

'What is it?'

He threw one at her. 'Acorns.'

She caught it. 'But that tree's been dead for centuries.'

The acorns were green and fresh. Coming over, Hannah looked at them and said, 'We should take one and plant it. You never know. It would be good, if it grew. Sort of keeping the tree alive.'

Josh laughed but Sulis took one of the seeds and crouched down. She made a hole with her finger, prodding down into the soft soil, and dropped the acorn in. 'Grow,' she said.

Driving back, Simon sat in the passenger seat, and soon fell asleep, snoring softly. Hannah hummed to herself as she drove, and turned up the music on the radio. Josh read the leaflet, curled in a huddle.

Sulis looked out of the window. As the car came over the downs, she saw the city below them in its secret hollow, lit up with streetlights, its streets gathered round the sacred spring like guardians.

She was sorry Caitlin had died. But she would never look over her shoulder again.

And she might even tell Josh her real name.

Zac

My master's funeral took place on a cold windy day in the church where he had once been married.

It was a sombre service. All the dignitaries of the council sent their carriages. Some of them even came themselves. Ralph Alleyn arranged everything. He was a true friend; I have never seen a man so devastated; he looked older sitting there in his pew, & he seemed lost in memories. The church was crowded with ladies of fashion & gentleman of influence, & I cursed each & every one of them with bitter venom as I sat there, because their city would benefit from Forrest's work, & yet they had despised him always.

Sylvia did not come.

She kept to her room, & Mrs Hall bought her a black dress. I was afraid she would leave in the night, that she might run away, because her grief was so great.

I knew what she was thinking. That her own rashness had killed him.

It was foolish, of course. He climbed the scaffolding every day, & his asthma had been worsening for years, but I could understand her agony. She had loved him very much, in ways I had no experience of.

As for me, I felt anger, & shame. I had despised him, & yet now all I could think of was his kindness & his temper & his obsessions. Did it take the man's death to make me know that I loved him too? Was I so dull that I had not seen it before?

There was one thing I could do, one thing I could mend, & I did it, working deep into the night after the funeral, the plans spread before me on his worktable.

Carefully, line by line, I restored his masterpiece. Compton might have the originals, but these would be identical, & so I removed all my stupid iregularities & the changes in measurements I had imagined to be so subtle. Gradually the drawing of the Circus regained its perfect proportions. The lamp shed a pool of light on me as I worked, & all around me the house slept, the rooms empty. Only once in Sylvia's room above did a board creak, as if she was awake & moving around . . .

I must have slept, afterwards.

Because I was woken by a shake of the arm.

'Zac! Wake up.'

The sun had risen. Its watery rays were streaming through the window. My neck was stiff & I found myself lying slumped on my arms, the plans under my head. I groaned, dizzy. 'What time is it?'

'Seven. Mrs Hall will be down soon. I made you this.'

It was a cup of chocolate, steaming & sweet. I gulped it down & felt its sweetness waken me in an instant. As I drank it she gazed down at the plans. 'Have you finished?'

'Yes.' I wiped my mouth. 'How did you know I was here?'

She managed the ghost of her cheeky smile. 'Heard you. I came down & peeped in a few times, but you were so intent on your work.'

I put the cup down. 'No one will ever know. One day these papers will be in a museum. *Jonathan Forrest's designs for the King's Circus*. People will marvel at their beauty & skill. That's all I can do for him now.'

'Maybe not all.'

I looked up, rolling the filmy papers together. The black dress made her look too pale, her hair gathered back. The redness had gone from her eyes, but I was sure she had eaten very little for days. 'What do you mean?'

'There was a message. Mr Forrest's son has come home. His ship docked at Bristol & he is on his way here now.'

I stared at her. Then I said, 'Oh.'

'Will he turn us out?'

I had no idea. 'I've never met him. He might . . . end my apprenticeship. Or he might keep me on until the Circus is finished.' I did not want to think about what would happen to her. Whatever sort of man Forrest's son was, he was not his father.

'Sylvia . . .'

'There's something else.' She was looking down at the plan, her mouth stubborn. 'The metopes.'

'What about them? I don't suppose . . .'

'We must add them. Indicate where they'll go. Or his design won't be as he wanted it.'

She picked up the drawings of the metopes & spread them on the table, & we looked at them. They were a mystery to me. If these emblems and images were the words of a story, they were in some language I could not read.

'I don't know what they mean. What order they go in . . .'

'It doesn't matter.' She took up a pencil. 'Number them. Put them on the plan. Before anyone can say they cost too much, or they're not needed. If they are a code, someone else will have to break it.'

So I numbered the metopes. I even left in the one I had drawn, of a tree struck by lightning, one great bough broken on the ground. Forrest's coat of arms was the oak, & now he was dead. What memorial could be better?

Just as we were finishing there was a clatter outside the house; Mrs Hall came down the stairs. We heard voices & her cry of recognition.

'Quick,' Sylvia whispered. We stacked the papers in a tidy pile, & I arranged the desk as it should be. As Forrest had left it. Then we turned.

A young man was standing in the doorway. For a

274

moment, I confess, my heart made a great foolish leap because if Forrest had returned from death looking twenty years younger, this was him.

The same dark eyes. The same quick, all-seeing look. Sylvia bobbed a slow curtsey. I bowed.

He said, 'You must be Zac.'

'Yes, sir. Welcome home.'

He nodded. 'Not the welcome I had hoped for.' He looked tired from the journey. He glanced round, as if he still expected to see his father there, in the old room. Then he smiled at Sylvia. 'My father wrote to me about you.'

In that instant I understood she would be safe.

She said, 'Master Forrest was the best man I ever knew.'

John Forrest the Younger smiled sadly. 'He was indeed. I think we were all lucky to know him.'

He was young, but he worked hard. In the next few days he was everywhere in the city, meeting Ralph Alleyn, talking to the workmen, encouraging the contractors. Work on the Circus was not allowed to slacken. Every day I saw the golden stones being cut & squared & shaped, the houses rising. I worked at his side, my jacket off, my linen sleeves rolled up out of the dirt, quite changed from what I was. And every night when we went home Sylvia & Mrs Hall laid a great meal for us.

I worked every hour I could. I worked like an animal works, without thinking. I didn't want to think, because then I would remember Forrest.

But one evening, when the workers had gone & I thought myself alone, someone coughed at my elbow. I turned & saw George Fisher.

He said, 'Mazter Vorrest wants you, zirr.'

There was something strange in the way he spoke the name. I said, 'Where is he?'

'In the chamber.'

We were silent a moment among the moonlit houses. Then I got up & followed him.

I had not been down to the secret chamber since the night Forrest had died. I suppose I hoped I would never have to see it again. To my surprise Sylvia was there, wrapped in her cloak, looking a little scared.

'Zac . . . What's going on?'

'I have no idea,' I said.

The space was empty. One candle flickered in the dark. Only the spring in the floor bubbled. But in the ground at its side a grave had been cut. And a stone lay next to it . . . A metope. It showed Bladud flying, his wings wide.

'There be one extra, somehow.' Fisher looked at me, expressionless. 'Zo it's to be here. For him.'

I stepped closer, & looked down. Sylvia clung on my arm.

We saw his coffin lying deep, with the serpent cut into the wood, and the circle and the triangle over it. Only for a second, in the flicker of the candle.

As I turned, Jack Forrest came along the passage with

Ralph Alleyn at his back. They both gazed down at the dark opening.

A few workmen waited outside, tools in their hands.

'It's as he wanted,' Alleyn said quietly. 'But no one will know. Except us.'

Jack Forrest looked at us. 'This morning I read my father's will. His wishes are clear, & I intend to honour them. He wished that Master Stoke's apprenticeship be completed, & that means, if you agree, Zac, you'll be working with me from now on.'

I nodded, not trusting myself to speak.

He looked at Sylvia. 'My father has also instructed that a house in the Circus is to be bought for you. And he has left you a small legacy.'

She was staring at the floor. 'I don't deserve it.'

'He thought you did.'

'He wrote that before he knew about me. What I really was.'

If she was not careful she would give us both away. I said quickly, 'Sylvia, it does not matter. He raced like a madman up those ladders to save you, & he knew then . . . He knew everything. But it didn't stop him. He still cared for your life. If he was here he'd laugh at you now & say, "Do as I say." Wouldn't he?'

She knew I was right. And I saw in her face that she would accept his gift, & that she would make the house a beautiful thing, because it had been his & he had given it to her. As for me, I had mixed feelings. Did I even like this tanned, earnest young Forrest? He seemed to have none of his father's dreams & visions. Once they had irritated me. Now I felt I could not live without them.

Ralph Alleyn said, 'We are to seal up this chamber. So take a last look around. Perhaps no one will ever come here again.'

I glanced at the walls, the corbelled ceiling. It was not a place I wanted to remember, or would think of easily. All my life it would be here, dark & silent, in the heart of my past.

Sylvia took a few steps to the spring. She leaned over & looked into the tiny pool of water, & through the steam I saw her reflection, rippled & blurred. Then she knelt. 'What's that?'

She put her fingers deep into the hot mud & dug out a tiny piece of paper, folded & broken & aged. It seemed to have been pushed up from somewhere deep by the seeping water.

We gathered round her as she unfolded it, but the pieces fell apart in her fingers.

'Bring the lantern.'

As Fisher held up the light we saw words on the fragment. She read them aloud, in a whisper. *I want you to end the shadow on my life.*

For a moment the room took the words & echoed them. Alleyn said, 'How did that come here?'

I glanced at him. If he *is* one of the Oroboros, he would surely know.

'It is a votive, thrown in the spring. Who knows where or how long ago? My father said there must be a whole series of waterways underlying this city.' Jack Forrest turned. 'Keep it, Sylvia. But now the men are waiting.'

They made the ground smooth & built up the arch as we watched, expertly raising the masonry so that the dim interior disappeared slowly, a steamy darkness becoming finally as small as the gap for the last stone, the keystone. As Fisher raised it, I put out my hand to stop him. 'Let me.'

He glanced at Forrest, who nodded, surprised.

I was an awkward workman. I slid the stone carefully into the gap, so that a ripple of mortar oozed out & dropped on to my shirt. Taking the trowel I scraped the stone clean, & stood back.

'Tis customary to make your mark.' Fisher gave me a small chisel & mallet, & for a moment I had no idea what he meant. The men grinned at each other.

Then I lifted the tools, & chipped Z S 1754 into the stone.

It looked like the work of a complete amateur.

Later, as I stood watching Alleyn take Sylvia home, Jack Forrest came up behind me & said, 'There's something I want to show you, Zac.'

We walked across the site, westward. The sun had set & the first stars were just coming out, faint among the clouds. A crescent moon hung over the hillside, &

somewhere sheep bleated, though I could not see them yet. On the far side there was a track leading to the fields, but I knew it would be a street very soon, one of the three that would lead from the Circus. At its end was a smooth rising slope of downland, & it was here the sheep were, & some pigs too, rooting under the oak trees that grew below.

Forrest stopped & leaned on the gate. 'This is it.'

'A field?'

'My field.' He looked up. 'You worked with my father. He was a very brilliant man, a man of sparks & fire … Have you ever thought what it must be like to be the son of Jonathan Forrest?'

Difficult, I thought, but I said nothing.

He waved his hand. 'The Circus is my father's masterpiece, but I intend to build my own, right here. His was the sun. Mine will be the moon. A great crescent of stone. You and I will build it, Zac, druidic symbols rising in a perfect city.'

I said, 'I would be honoured,' but in fact my gaze was on his hand. Around his smallest finger he wore a ring, & the ring was gold. It was in the shape of a snake that devoured its own tail.

Perhaps he saw me looking, for in a low voice he said, 'He left it to me. You need not have worried about the metopes. I would have made sure they were included.'

We looked at each other.

Below us, where the trees were, all the jackdaws rose & karked & resettled, as if they were not yet ready to sleep.

Author's Note

I have always been fascinated by the King's Circus at Bath. The whole city has a peculiarly golden air, a sense of mysteries around corners, but this circular street intrigues by its completeness, and its strange symbolic carvings. I wasn't surprised that its architect, John Wood the Elder, was influenced by druidic theories and ideas of sacred measurement.

I wanted to experiment a little in this novel; to wrap three strands of story around each other, so that they never quite touch, but echo themes and images. I used some of the realities of John Wood's life, but changed things and invented others, so that Jonathan Forrest is a fictional creation, based only partly on fact. Bladud is mythical; his tale can be found in old chronicles. And Sulis is a story of my own.

Myth, fiction, fact. The three points of the triangle. One turns into another, so that what the truth is is never wholly certain. I hope this novel has captured some of that enigma, that circling around events and places. And I hope, one day, that you who read it will visit the Waters of Sulis for yourselves.

Catherine Fisher